KILLING ME SOFTLY

JULIE MULHERN

J & M PRESS

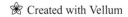 Created with Vellum

Liz, Laurie, and Jen, your endless patience is endlessly appreciated. Thank you.

Edie, this was fun. Let's do it again soon!

CHAPTER ONE

June 1975
Kansas City, Missouri

"Ellison Walford Russell, have you lost your ever-loving mind?" Mother's whisper-yell was less like a whisper, more like a yell.

Heads turned.

Realizing she'd attracted unwanted attention, she lowered her voice. "Have you taken leave of your senses?"

"Jones," I told her.

"What?" Her brow furrowed and she stared at me as if, as she suggested, I'd lost my mind.

"It's Ellison Walford Jones. Not, Russell."

"Details." She dismissed my second marriage with an elegant flick of her wrist. "You cannot do this."

My brilliant husband had suggested that Mother and I discuss the latest additions to our household in a public place. Anarchy was a homicide detective and made his living studying people, their emotions, and their reactions. He'd predicted Mother might react strongly. And he'd been right. Mother and I were seated at a small table at La Bonne Bouchée, a table so close to the other small tables that eavesdropping was inevitable. In a more private setting she'd already be detailing my failings as a Walford and a daughter. Oh, and she'd also question my intelligence (not just my sanity) or melt my face with her wholly terrifying death glare.

Fortunately for me, we were at a café where we knew at least a third of the women clustered around the small tables, so Mother forced a Lord-give-me-patience smile and took another tiny sip from her demitasse cup. "Obviously, you haven't thought this through."

The decision to welcome Beau and his dog, Finn, into our home was made in an instant. And felt absolutely right.

"Isn't Karma staying with you this summer? Where will you put everyone?" Mother was clutching at straws.

"I have plenty of bedrooms."

"You have gallery openings coming up. You don't have time to raise someone else's child." Mother had never shown an ounce of interest in my career. And she wasn't interested now. My painting was just an excuse to send Beau away.

"I'll manage." I broke off a tiny piece of palmier and popped it into my mouth. Sweet. Buttery. Were it not for their flaky crumbs that decorated my lap whenever I indulged, palmiers would be the perfect pastry.

"Ellison, this is a bad idea."

This wasn't an abstract idea. This was a little boy. One who needed me. Giving him a home was a fabulous idea.

"You'll fall in love with that child, then someone will claim him—either his aunt or Whit Riley—and you'll be crushed."

I'd hate it if Beau left us. My heart might shatter. But Beau had been through enough. He deserved some goodness. "If that happens, I'll manage. In the meantime, he'll have a safe, stable, caring home."

"You're impossible." Her emotions played across her face—annoyance, impatience, and reluctant acceptance. "Was it necessary to drag me down here?"

"I don't know what you mean." I knew exactly what she meant.

She arched an elegant brow. "The next time you're counting on an audience to quell my tongue, ask me for lunch at the club." Mother wrinkled her nose as if the smell of delicious coffee and French pastries was unpleasant. "The Plaza isn't what it once was. In my day, we dressed to come here. Not anymore. This morning, on the sidewalk, I saw a couple." She leaned forward and lowered her voice, "They were hippies. Her shorts were so short I could practically see her cheeks. His hair was longer than hers. And they had their hands in each other's back pockets." She sat back in her chair with a what's-the-world-coming-to grimace on her face.

I offered up an apologetic smile. "I have a million errands on the Plaza." The Country Club Plaza was my favorite place to shop. There was Swanson's and Woolf Brothers and Harzfeld's, and now that Anarchy and I were married, Jack Henry for men's clothes.

"Errands?" She didn't believe me.

"Alterations to pick up from Swanson's and Woolf's. I had a pair of pumps resoled, and I have a sweater at Plaza Weavers. I need to buy the next book for my book club at Bennett Schneider, then stop by the drugstore. Oh, I also have to drop off Grace's library books."

Mother sniffed. Mollified?

I didn't dare ask.

"I expect you to take me to the furniture maker you found." The furniture maker was Aaron Minton, and he was married to Beau's aunt. Aaron had a studio in Raytown, a place Mother would never dream of visiting without a compelling reason. "Thursday suits me."

"I'm free all day." I hid behind a bite of palmier, hoped most of the crumbs landed on my napkin, and searched for a new topic. "How's Elaine Sandingham?" Elaine was one of the many women with whom Mother played bridge.

"She's a wreck." Elaine's husband, Owen, had recently died. "Owen ran every aspect of their lives. I don't know how Elaine will manage. At least he died in his sleep."

"We should all be so lucky." I pictured Owen Sandingham, a man in his late sixties who played both tennis and golf. He also swam, often arriving at the pool while I was swimming my early morning laps. "He seemed very fit to just die in his sleep."

"Are you suggesting he was murdered?" The chill in Mother's voice could bring on the next ice age.

"No. Not at all." I held up fingers-spread-wide, not-remotely-suggesting-murder hands. "I'm just saying he seemed active and fit and full of life."

Mollified that I wasn't suggesting murder, Mother donned a suitably sad expression. "It's a shame he's gone. My heart goes out to Elaine."

"When is the funeral?"

"Thursday morning. Your father has a business meeting he can't cancel, so you can accompany me to the funeral. After the reception, we'll head to—" another disdainful sniff "—Raytown."

I'd walked right into that one. I was going to a funeral. Whether I wanted to or not. "What time should I pick you up?"

"I'll drive. The service begins at eleven, so be ready by ten-fifteen. There's a reception at the club immediately following."

"Frances." Joanne Woodfield stood next to our table. "Ellison."

I stood, showering the floor with palmier crumbs. "Mrs.

Woodfield, how nice to see you." Joanne lived on the next block down from mine, the second house from the corner.

"Please, sit." She waved with vigor, as if the airflow could make me reclaim my chair. "You make me feel old."

I didn't budge.

"I insist."

Mother gave a tiny nod, and I sat.

"I'm sorry to interrupt, but I wanted to ask Ellison about the Dixons' house. Have you heard anything? Such an eyesore."

My across-the-street neighbors, Marian and Leonard Dixon, had gone on vacation. In their absence, their house had burned, and no one had been able to reach them for almost two weeks. Between the fire, the fire hoses, the firemen's axes, and the damage caused by a few days of relentless rain, the place was a total loss.

"The Dixons are home. I'm sure one of them has called their insurance company." I wasn't remotely sure of that. As far as I could tell, Leonard had left Marian (on my front stoop). He'd driven away, and I wasn't sure he'd stopped until the car's gas gauge read empty. Did Marian have the wherewithal to pick up the phone and call their insurance agent? An important question, for which I had no answer.

"Will they rebuild?" she asked.

I had my doubts, what with Leonard taking off for parts unknown. "I don't know."

"The place is a hazard. I've seen neighborhood children poking around the wreckage."

I made a note to tell Beau to steer clear.

"What are you going to do?" Joanne demanded.

"Me?" Was she serious?

"You live across the street."

Which in no way made me responsible. "I can't file a claim for the Dixons."

"But you can talk to Marian."

In Marian's mind, proximity to me had caused the fire that destroyed her house. Crazy? Yes. Especially since the police had arrested the person responsible for the blaze. But Marian never let facts interfere with emotions. The woman was several crates short of a full load. "I doubt Marian wants to speak with me. Try Jane Carson." Jane had taken in Marian's cat, Percival, after the fire.

"I'll do that." Joanne gave a brief nod. "Frances, how's Harrington?"

"Fine, thank you. Lee?"

"I hardly see him. Between work and the golf course, the man is never home."

Mother's eyes dulled with a heard-this-story-a-million-times boredom. "When do you leave for...where is it you go?"

"Kiawah. We're flying to South Carolina the day after swim championships. Our grandson is having a good season, and we're hoping he wins his races."

"How long will you stay?" I asked. With Marian gone, Mother would be looking for a new spy, and Joanne lived close. An extended vacation was in my best interest.

"Through the end of September."

My heart soared. "How lovely for you."

"Have you visited the low country?"

"Just Charleston," I replied.

"It's a beautiful city, but Lee and I love a beach. We bought our place as an investment years ago." She offered me a satisfied smirk. "The rent for June covers the mortgage for the year."

"I keep telling Ellison she needs a vacation home."

Since when? That topic had never, ever been up for discussion. I stared across the table at Mother and wondered what had prompted my sudden need for a second home.

"Imagine my surprise when she started looking at Tuscan villas."

Anarchy and I had never, ever considered buying a villa. I enjoyed visiting different places too much.

Joanne turned her attention my way. "Did you find anything?"

"Not yet." I'd play Mother's game. "Finding the perfect place will take multiple trips."

"Can your husband take that much time off work?" A healthy dose of snide lurked in Joanne's voice.

"We're in no hurry," I replied. Did she mean to be offensive?

Mother brought her demi-tasse cup to her pursed lips. "You realize Anarchy doesn't have to work? He did graduate from Stanford."

Joanne lifted a brow. "Did he? Yet, he chooses to mix with the dregs of society."

Wow. Just…wow. I laced my fingers together and hid my hands in my lap. My husband had a strict moral code. There was right. And there was wrong. And murder was wrong. "He wants victims and their families to get some modicum of justice."

Joanne scratched the back of her neck. "Does he need a degree from Stanford for that? Surely he could put his education to better use."

I offered up a frigid smile and crafted the perfect put-down, one that would leave Joanne reeling. It didn't come easy. It didn't come at all.

"So nice seeing you, Joanne." Mother shifted in her chair, and shot me a glare, almost as if she could see the rude cogs spinning in my brain. "We'll have to meet for drinks soon."

Joanne was officially dismissed. But she wasn't going without a fight. "It's hard to drag Lee off the golf course this time of year. He's a scratch golfer, you know."

Mother gave a regal nod. "I heard something about Lee's golf. Didn't you, Ellison?"

Lee's golf? I was still trying to craft the perfect come-back. Why was Mother asking me questions? Like a rabbit caught between two wolves, I froze. Maybe they'd forget me if I stayed very still.

Mother nodded as if I'd agreed with her. Then she smiled at Joanne. A predator's smile. "It's posted in the ladies' locker room, but I don't know if you've seen it—Ellison holds the low-round title at the club."

"Yes, but she plays off the ladies' tees."

Oh dear Lord. This needed to end. "It was so nice seeing you, Mrs. Whitfield. If I see Jane, I'll be sure and mention your concerns."

"Thank you, Ellison." With a brief nod to Mother, she left us.

Mother loosed a dramatic sign. "That woman."

"I thought you were friends."

"We are."

"An Italian villa?"

"I did not want to hear about her beach house for the fiftieth time. One-upmanship was the best option." Mother tapped her chin with the tip of a perfectly manicured finger. "An Italian villa isn't a bad idea. You could find your bodies someplace other than Kansas City."

"I haven't found a body in weeks."

She directed a chilling glare my way. "Are you trying to jinx yourself?"

"ELLISON, THIS FUNERAL WILL BE STANDING ROOM ONLY." Mother scowled at me. "I've been waiting for ages."

Two minutes. She'd waited for two minutes. I'd seen her pull up.

"I had to get out of the car and ring the bell." She ran her gaze over my navy dress, conservative pumps, and pearls. Unable to find fault, she shifted her gaze to her Mercedes. "Come along. We're already late."

If thirty minutes early was late. I hurried down the front steps, slipped into the passenger seat, and buckled up.

"Worried about my driving?"

"Not in the least." Totally. Mother didn't believe in defensive driving. It was the other driver's duty to stay out of her way. I didn't point out that she'd been injured in a car accident that wasn't her fault not long ago. I valued my head's connection to my shoulders. "Everyone should wear seatbelts."

"They wrinkle my clothes."

Who was I to argue?

We arrived at the church early enough to find a spot in the lot.

"We're halfway to Arkansas," Mother complained.

We'd parked two rows from the door.

"Hurry up, Ellison. I hate sitting in the back."

Dutifully, I followed her into the church, where we had our choice of rows near the front.

Mother selected an aisle seat in the fifth row and forced me to climb over her.

I sank into the pew and glanced over my shoulder.

"Tacky, Ellison."

I returned my gaze to the altar.

"Who's here?"

"You just told me looking was tacky."

"It is, but the damage is done. Who did you see?"

"Liz and Perry Brandt."

She gave a small nod. "Who else?"

"Julie and Robbie Smart."

"Who else?"

We could play this game ad nauseum. "Are you looking for someone in particular?"

"No."

"Joanne Woodfield is here."

"Is Lee with her?"

"I didn't see him."

A tiny smile touched Mother's lips. "Perhaps he's playing golf. What's Grace doing today?"

"Junior golf, then she's spending the afternoon at the pool." Children had the run of the course on Thursday mornings. If Lee Whitfield was playing golf, he hadn't teed off yet.

"And the boy?"

"His name is Beau."

"What's he doing?"

"The same."

"Running up your club bill."

"He's charging to the Rileys' account."

"Ellison, you haven't thought this through. What about tuition?"

"There's plenty of money."

"Whose?"

We were in the process of getting Beau's DNA tested. The answer would determine which trust supported him. "It doesn't matter. I have plenty of money."

"Which should go to Grace."

The organist played the first notes of *The Strife is O'er*. If only that were true of this conversation.

We listened, dry-eyed, to the readings, the eulogy, and Owen's brother, who spoke at length about how much Owen enjoyed living. His remarks had Elaine sobbing into a lace-edged handkerchief.

The service ended, and Mother and I drove to the reception at the club. She sped up the winding drive. "Very nice service," she observed. "I'd give it an eight out of ten."

She scored funerals? Why was I even surprised? Mother rated everything. Weddings, wedding gowns, the flowers in the church, and wedding cakes (How moist? How sweet? The cake to icing ratio). She rated debutante dresses and curtsies. But funerals? Wasn't it enough to say it was a lovely service and leave the competitions to the living?

"What kept it from being a ten?" I asked. I couldn't help myself.

"Owen's brother talked too long, and Elaine cried too much."

"So if she'd been stoic, you'd have given it a nine?"

"There's no need to be flippant."

"It's a serious question."

One which she ignored. "Let's see how they do with the reception. Your father and I attended Paul Wilder's funeral and reception, and Lila served call liquor. I guarantee you Paul was spinning in his casket. Like a top. The man always drank the good stuff." Mother shook her head in disapproval. "Did she think we wouldn't notice?"

"Maybe she worried about the cost."

"Then have the reception in the church basement and serve cookies and coffee. If you're going to do something, do it right. And that means serving good liquor. When I die, I want the best. If you cut any corners, I'll come back and haunt you."

That was a terrifying thought.

We stepped into the reception, and Liz Brandt claimed my arm. "May I steal Ellison for a moment, Mrs. Walford?"

Mother approved of Liz and offered her an almost-warm smile. "Of course."

Liz pulled me away.

"Thank you. More than you can know."

"Your eye was twitching."

"Was it? Already?" I sighed. "We're together for the rest of the afternoon."

"Oh?"

"We're going furniture shopping after the reception."

"Where?" she asked.

"A studio in Raytown."

An amused smile curled Liz's lips. "Frances is going to Raytown?"

"Come by the house and see the desk we bought for Anarchy." It was gorgeous. A work of art. Definitely worth stepping off the beaten path. Mother liked the desk well enough to venture far east of her usual stomping grounds.

"I will." She glanced at the widow, who was accepting condolences. "Poor Elaine. Owen's death has come as such a shock."

"To everyone."

"I heard a heart attack."

"That's what I heard." I made a sad, thirsty sound, and we walked to the bar. I surveyed the top-shelf bottles and said, "Mother will be pleased."

"With what?"

"They're pouring the good stuff."

Liz ordered a gin and tonic with two limes.

"The usual, Mrs. Jones?" The bartender flashed me a grin. He already knew my daytime order.

"A white wine spritzer, please."

He nodded as if I'd lived up to his expectations.

With our drinks in hand, Liz and I took in the rapidly filling room.

"Good turnout," Liz observed.

"He was well liked. And young." The more one aged, the thinner the funeral turnout. "Are you traveling this summer?"

"Perry has a trial in late July. We're stuck here till it's over. I guess I could head to Colorado alone, but it just wouldn't be a vacation without him."

"There you are." Libba lifted a martini glass in greeting. "Liz, you look fabulous. As always." Like me, Liz wore a navy-blue dress. Hers was a linen sheath that she'd paired with multiple gold chains.

I tilted my head and stared at my best friend. As a rule, she didn't attend funerals. She found them depressing. But she'd donned a conservative black dress and dug out her pearls for the occasion. "I'm surprised to see you here."

Libba gave a tiny, resigned shrug. "Charlie was Owen's doctor."

"Really?" Liz's eyes sparkled with unsatiated curiosity. "Do tell, what killed him?"

"Not Charlie." Too quick. Too sharp. Libba was on the defensive.

I couldn't help but wonder why.

CHAPTER TWO

"Is there a reason these people located their business in Raytown?"

These people. I tightened my grip on the steering wheel of Mother's Mercedes. "They found a warehouse that worked for their needs."

"The first rule of real estate is location, location, location." Mother cast her judgmental gaze out the window and caught sight of a disreputable burger shack. Her shoulders gave an involuntary shudder. "Are you sure you know where you're going?"

I did not reply.

"Ellison?"

"I know where I'm going." Sort of.

Mother's gaze lingered on the burger shack. "When you next talk to your father, ask him how long it's been since he saw the doctor."

I glanced at Mother. "Is there something I should know?"

"Don't be so dramatic. I've told him to go. More than once. If I mention it again, I'll be a nag."

Returning my focus to the road, I nodded. "Fine. I'll ask. Is there a specific reason you're worried?"

"Owen."

That made sense. If Elaine could lose her husband, anyone could. But Daddy didn't have any health problems. That I knew of, but I wouldn't put it past my parents to clam up about anything less than perfect health. I forced the sudden rush of worry into a box and hid it on a dark shelf in the back closet of my mind.

"Also, if I'm not around, the man eats French fries and ice cream for dinner.

The worry box required another large shove. "I'll talk to him."

"Thank you."

"I noticed Elaine poured good liquor."

A dismissive noise rumbled in Mother's throat. "Did you see the buffet? Egg salad."

The club had served a variety of finger sandwiches, crudité, house-made potato chips, fresh fruit, and gazpacho. They'd also served lemon bars, lime tarts, raspberry mousse, and pot de crème. A nice spread by any standard.

Any standard but Mother's. Frances Walford was not a fan of egg-salad sandwiches. The other delicious finger sandwiches on the buffet, chicken salad, cucumber, watercress, and salmon, were eclipsed by the presence of egg. To Mother's way of thinking, lowly egg salad should not be served to guests. Ever.

"Overall score?" I shouldn't play along with her scoring game, but I couldn't help it.

"Eight for the funeral. Eight for the reception. Nine, but for the egg salad." Deep lines cut from the edges of Mother's nose to the corners of her lips. "Just how far away is this place?"

"Not far now."

One wrong turn (thank heavens Mother didn't notice) and a few minutes later, I pulled into the small parking lot next to the warehouse that housed Minton's Fine Furniture.

"This is it?" Mother's disapproval dripped, relentless as a leaky faucet. *Plink, plink, plink.*

She was the one who asked to come. I took a deep breath and held it for a long second. "Don't judge a book by its cover. It's what's inside that matters."

"For a grown woman, you're incredibly naïve. Everyone judges books by their covers. If the cover is unappealing, most will never crack the spine."

She wasn't wrong. But I refused to cede her point. On principle. Substance mattered. "What about *Watership Down?*" The cover was a boring white with an uninspired drawing of a compass and a rabbit. "Half the country is reading about a fluffle of rabbits."

She frowned at me. "Pardon?"

"A group of rabbits is called a 'fluffle.'"

Her frown deepened, and she tilted her head and stared at me as if I'd lost my mind. I received that exact look from her on a regular basis.

"My point is that you'll appreciate what's inside." I opened the car door, and the soles of my shoes crunched against pea gravel that filled a crater in the crumbling concrete.

Mother carefully picked her way across the parking lot's uneven pavement to the building's entrance. She took in the faded paint and steel door and her nose wrinkled in extreme distaste. "You take me to the nicest places. Is there a bowling alley nearby? Perhaps a greasy spoon diner or a tattoo parlor? Ellison's tour of places one should never go? I should have dressed for the occasion." She smoothed the lapel of her navy Guy Laroche suit.

My hands clenched in annoyance. She was the one who'd insisted I bring her here. "Just wait till you get inside. I know the exterior isn't what you're used to, but Aaron's craftsmanship— his artistry— more than make up for the first impression." Or the neighborhood. Or the disintegrating parking lot.

Aaron welcomed us with a warm smile.

Mother tilted her head and gazed up at him, seemingly unimpressed with his size or his leather apron. "My daughter says you're a genius."

He grinned. The man had dimples. "I wouldn't go that far."

"Look at his work, Mother. Then decide for yourself."

She sighed. Dramatically. As if I'd dragged her to Raytown against her will. Maybe once, possibly twice in her whole lifetime had Mother done something she didn't want to do. And on those rare-as-a-blue-moon occasions, it definitely wasn't her daughters who'd forced her. "Fine," she huffed. "Show me."

Thirty minutes later, Mother had selected new end tables for her living room and commissioned a bedroom set, and the expression on her face had morphed from what-is-that-appalling-smell to that of a cat who'd caught three canaries.

Aaron sat behind a beautiful pecan desk, added up a list of numbers, and quoted her a price.

Mother's lips twitched—just slightly—as if she couldn't believe her luck and an actual smile might double the price of her new furniture.

"Will you take a check?" she asked.

"Of course."

"You'll deliver the tables?"

Aaron's dimples reappeared. "Absolutely."

"When will the bedroom set be ready?"

"Six weeks."

Mother took out her checkbook. "To whom shall I make the check payable?

"Minton's Fine Furniture. The tables, plus a fifty percent deposit?"

In her elegant script, Mother wrote a check for the full amount and handed it to Aaron. "You're married to Virginia Wycliff."

Aaron winced. "Minton now."

Mother returned her checkbook to her handbag and snapped the clasp. "Where is she?"

"Visiting her mother at Pleasant Lane."

Mother could hardly find fault with Virginia for visiting her mother. She tapped her tastefully manicured fingers against Aaron's desk. "She's aware she has a nephew?"

Aaron shot me a panicked look. "She's aware."

Mother hinged back in her chair. "And what does she plan to do about it?"

I'd told Virginia about Beau. She'd told me that she didn't want to move Beau to Raytown and take him away from his friends and the life he'd always known. She'd also told me that she and Aaron had never wanted children. They would be at a loss as to caring for a boy whose world had imploded. I'd felt nothing but relief at her admission.

Aaron tugged at his apron straps. "If Beau is happy, we don't want to upset him."

"Sometimes what's best for a child isn't their happiness."

Oh dear Lord. Did she honestly believe that? "Mother, this is none of your business."

The shock on her face—it was as if I'd slapped her. "If that boy is staying with you, it is definitely my business." She glanced at Aaron, then scowled at me. A deep scowl. Then she rose from her chair, a signal that she was ready to leave. "Ellison, we will discuss this in the car."

Oh, joy. I couldn't wait. It was going to be a long ride home.

WITH A NEW MOUTH TO FEED, AGGIE HAD UPPED HER DINNER ante. Gone were grilled chicken breasts or white fish filets paired with asparagus or haricots verts and a salad. Waistline-conscious dinners that Grace and I preferred (and Anarchy endured). Instead, Aggie seemed determined to tempt the boy who'd lost his appetite. Tonight she'd served barbequed pulled pork with a mustard and vinegar sauce that was completely foreign to my tomato-based Kansas City palate, macaroni and cheese, and creamy coleslaw.

Aggie stood in the doorway from the kitchen, wearing a muumuu as bright as a Hawaiian sunset and a hopeful smile. "I made peach pie for anyone who finishes their dinner."

Beau pushed the macaroni around his plate without eating a bite.

With a disheartened shake of her head, Aggie returned to the kitchen.

"How was swim practice this afternoon?" I asked. "Championships will be here before we know it."

Grace side-eyed Beau. When he remained silent, she answered me. "Practice was fine."

Wow. I'd hoped that would be more of a conversation starter. "Any plans for the weekend?" I asked Grace.

"I thought I'd just hang out around here."

"If you don't have plans, we could go to the farm," I suggested. "There's fishing and swimming and horseback riding. Do you ride Beau?"

"I learned at camp." Camp. Beau was supposed to leave for camp in July. Did we dare send him when he wasn't eating, when he seemed wan despite his tanned skin, when the light in his eyes had dulled to barely a flicker? Finn, the Airedale who moved in with Beau, nudged the boy's elbow as if encouraging him to actually lift the macaroni-laden fork to his mouth.

"Do you like horses?" I asked.

He shrugged. "I guess."

That was hardly a ringing endorsement for my plan. "The dogs will love it. They'll have acres to run, a pond for swimming, and rabbits to chase. Did you know a group of rabbits is called a fluffle?"

Beau put down his fork, and Finn whined softly.

"Why haven't you taken me to the farm?" Anarchy's voice was teasing.

Because he was so often busy catching killers. And when he wasn't, we already had plans. "The timing hasn't worked."

"I could do with a change of scenery, and aside from that weekend at the Fin and Feather, I've not spent much time in the country."

"Your parents didn't take you camping?" asked Grace.

Galaxies twinkled in Anarchy's coffee-brown eyes. "Grace, you've met my parents. They talk a good back-to-nature game, but a mosquito's whine can send them running."

"Should I call to make the arrangements?" Surely a change of scenery would be good for Beau? Anarchy held my gaze, then gave a tiny I-don't-have-a better-idea nod. "We can leave tomorrow after swim practice. You can skip Saturday morning." Few kids showed up for Saturday practices. Grace and Beau would not be missed.

"The farm will be fun." Grace sounded as if a weekend in the country was an experience to be endured, not a treat.

Ignoring the lack of enthusiasm, I smoothed the napkin in my lap. "Well, then—that's settled."

"Hey, Beau," Grace said.

He looked up from his uneaten dinner.

"Want to take the dogs for a walk when we're done?"

"I'm kinda tired." Beau seemed lost in a maze of sadness. No, not just sadness. I'd seen bemused rage shimmering in his eyes. And who could blame him?

"Anarchy and I will walk Max and Finn later." After the sun sank below the horizon. The temperature had flirted with the upper nineties, and I wanted the cool of the evening before I wrangled two large dogs.

"We could go to Brookside for ice cream," Grace offered.

"Whatever." Beau barely managed a shrug.

"Beau." I kept my tone gentle.

He looked at me with drooping eyes.

"How can we help you?"

His face shuttered.

"You're unhappy. Obviously. And it's okay to feel what you're feeling." Oh dear Lord, I sounded like a wacky granola-crunching guru. "Being sad is natural. Being angry is natural. But, you should know, we're glad you're here with us. And we're here whenever you need a shoulder or a punching bag."

His hand rose to his throat as if he suddenly found it hard to swallow. "May I please be excused?"

"No pie?" Surely peach pie would keep him at the table? He hadn't touched his dinner, but the boy needed to eat something. And I didn't much care if his calories came from sugar.

He shook his head. "No, thank you."

"Then, yes, you may be excused."

He and Finn left the table. Max, our Weimaraner, seemed torn. Follow his friends or keep a watchful eye on the plate of uneaten pork. His stomach won, and he sat.

"Way to go, Mom."

"What?"

"You made him cry."

My heart clenched at Grace's accusation. The very last thing I wanted to do was bring Beau more pain,

Anarchy took a sip from his water goblet. "It needed to be said, Grace."

"But not like that." She sounded as disapproving as Mother.

"Then how?" I asked. Someday Grace would be a mother, and she'd discover the job didn't come with an instruction manual. We all just muddled through as best we could.

"Maybe don't point out that he's been moping."

"So we should ignore that he's not eating and barely sleeping?"

"It's better than embarrassing him." Embarrassment, the worst thing that could happen to a teenager.

Except, it wasn't. Grace had endured much worse. Beau had, too. And the boy was barely ten.

Grace took the napkin from her lap and put it on the table next to her plate. "Look, you're worried. I get it. Let me talk to him."

"What will you say?" I asked.

She stood. "I'll tell him I know what it's like to lose a parent." Her gaze shifted to Anarchy. "And I know what it's like to find a new one."

A flush rose on my husband's tanned cheeks. "Thanks, Grace." His voice was thick.

She shrugged as if she hadn't just made his day. "It's true." She stood. "I'll talk to Beau."

The door swung shut behind her, and Anarchy whispered, "Wow."

I reached across that table and squeezed his hand. "She adores you. And she successfully ditched clearing the table."

Together we carried the dishes into the kitchen, and when the heat abated, we clipped leashes onto Max's and Finn's collars and headed outside.

The first star pricked the night sky, and I paused and made a wish.

Anarchy joined me in looking up at the sky. "Nice night."

"The French call this l'heure bleue, the blue hour." The dusk looked like velvet, and the air was a warm caress.

Anarchy reached for my free hand.

The evening was almost perfect. Almost. "What can we do for Beau?"

"I think we're doing it." He gave my fingers a quick squeeze. "Offer him support and acceptance and let him know we love having him share our home."

"He's a ten-year-old boy whose world just crashed down on him." Worry twisted my stomach. "He needs stability. I guarantee you he's wondering what happens next."

Finn looked over his shoulder to figure out why the man at the other end of his leash wasn't walking, but Anarchy didn't budge. "What do you want to happen?

Max, sensing an important moment, didn't pull on his leash. "I want to keep him." Whit wasn't kind, and Virginia lived in Raytown. Beau belonged with us.

"For the summer?"

"Forever." I stared at the sky and wished on a second star. A woman could never make too many wishes. "What do you want?"

"The same as you."

Relief wobbled my knees.

Anarchy's strong hand clasped my elbow. "You okay?"

I blinked away a veil of tears. "Never better."

"What's next?"

"We reach out to Whit." Unpleasant but doable. "We talk to Virginia."

"Okay."

"I guess we should talk to Beau first. What if he doesn't want us?"

The dogs huffed. Of course Beau wanted us. Whit was an ass, and Beau's aunt didn't want a child. Where else would he go?

"He'll want us." Anarchy agreed with the dogs.

"Then we hire a lawyer."

"Your mother."

The fly in the proverbial ointment. "What about her?"

"She's not a fan of the unconventional." Anarchy knew firsthand.

"You don't give her enough credit. She accepted Karma." That Daddy had fathered a child before marrying Mother had shocked us all. Especially Mother. But she'd risen to the occasion. And Karma was due to arrive from California on Monday. She'd stay with me until she found a house to buy. Jane Addison, a real estate agent with ties to the neighborhood, had volunteered to help my sister find the perfect home. Volunteered wasn't the right word, as Jane would earn a fat commission. I suspected she was rubbing gleeful hands together over how far San Francisco housing dollars would go in Kansas City.

"Ellison?"

"What? Sorry. I was thinking of Karma."

Max pulled on his leash; his patience had reached its end.

We walked.

"Do we send him to camp?" asked Anarchy.

"Let's see how this weekend goes. The change of scenery might do him good." A woman could hope. And wish on stars. I made a third wish.

Woof!

"Hush, Finn." The Airedale strained against Anarchy's hold.

"Sorry. It's me. This guy and I are old friends." Joanne Woodfield's husband, Lee, crouched next to Finn and rubbed the dog's ears. "So it's true?"

"What's true?"

"Beau Riley is staying with you."

A blissful expression, fully evident in the glow from the nearest streetlamp, relaxed Finn's face. His tail wagged as if it might never get another chance, and he groaned.

"It's true," I replied.

Lee stood and extended a hand to Anarchy. "I don't believe we've met. Lee Woodfield."

"Anarchy Jones."

Unhappy with the suspension of attention, Finn pawed at Lee's leg.

He crouched next to the demanding dog. "You're the homicide detective."

"That's right."

"From what Joanne tells me, you married a woman guaranteed to keep you working."

The muscles in my back tightened. "I find bodies. I don't kill people."

"I'm just teasing, Ellison."

His can't-you-take-a-joke tone grated my nerves. In my experience, people said they were joking after they'd said something offensive and someone called them out. "I understand you've been playing a lot of golf."

"So says the holder of the club record. Of course, you play from the ladies tee."

I was a decent golfer who'd had a great day—sixteen fairways, no bunkers, and I one-putted fifteen holes.

"The approaches, chips, and putts are the same." Anarchy's voice was cool, almost chilly.

"No argument here." Lee held up his hands, and Finn nudged his leg, urging him to resume his pets. "Are you a golfer, Anarchy?"

"Not for years."

"A shame. It's a great couples' sport."

Really? I'd never seen a club in his wife's hands. "Does Joanne play?"

"She says it's a good walk spoiled." His gaze shifted to Anarchy. "We'll have to get you out on the course."

"I need a few refresher lessons first."

"Get those lessons. We'll play a round." Lee squinted at his watch. "I should go. Joanne will wonder where I am." He strode into the darkness.

"Interesting guy."

A breeze tickled the back of my neck, and I shivered despite the heat.

"You okay?" Anarchy's hand on the small of my back chased away the sudden premonition.

"Fine." For now.

CHAPTER THREE

"Ellison!" Libba's voice climbed the stairs and rudely pushed past the open door to our bedroom. "Where are you?"

Max grumbled.

So did Anarchy. "What time is it?"

I glanced at the clock. "Not quite five-thirty."

"How did she get in?"

"Ellison!" Libba sounded as if she were in a tither, and Libba in a tither might climb into our bed to tell me her problem.

"I'd better go." I jammed my arms into a robe as I hurried toward my friend. "I'm coming!"

"There's no coffee," Libba wailed.

All she had to do was push the button and Mr. Coffee would fulfill her wishes. Aggie filled Mr. Coffee's reservoir each night so that he was ready in the morning. "Coming!" I heard a scratch from inside Beau's room and let Finn out.

He barreled down the back stairway on his way to the yard.

I stumbled into the kitchen a moment later, pushed Mr. Coffee's button, and let the dogs out. Then I turned to my friend

—my usually chic friend—and gasped. "What happened to you?"

Libba's hair was wild, but her eyes were wilder. She wore a wrinkled tee-shirt, a pair of jean shorts, and Dr. Scholl's sandals. No make-up. No jewelry. No insouciant air. She raked shaking fingers through her hair. "Charlie's kids did this."

"Did what?"

"This." She framed her face with spread fingers—she could stand in for Phyllis Diller. "They switched my pills."

I took two coffee mugs from the cabinet and put them on the counter. "Explain."

"They took my diet pills and put them in my sleeping pill bottle. I've been up all night."

"So you took diet pills before bed." I gave her a disapproving frown—women died from taking those pills.

"Don't judge. Not now. I haven't slept a wink. I figured the whole thing out around three this morning." Her left eye twitched. "Can I kill them? Is it justifiable homicide? Ask Anarchy."

The dogs scratched at the back door.

I let them in, dispensed treats, whispered a quick, heart-felt "thank you" to Mr. Coffee, then filled the coffee mugs. "You're sure it was Charlie's kids?"

"They were at my apartment yesterday. They did it."

"You have to tell Charlie." I handed her a mug.

Libba clutched her coffee like a lifeline. "I can't do that."

"Fooling with someone's medications could be dangerous."

"Don't I know it."

"Did they do anything else?"

She stared into her coffee as if the dark liquid held the secrets of the universe, then her shoulders shook as if a goose had walked over her grave. "They short sheeted my bed and slathered my toilet seat with cold cream."

The classics. Hardly worth a shudder. "You have to tell Charlie about the pills."

She groaned and sank onto a stool at the kitchen island. "He's been so stressed lately. I hate to add to it."

Switching medications, even diet pills, was dangerous. If she didn't tell him, I would. I said as much.

Libba set her coffee mug on the counter and ran her palms over her cheeks. "He's lost two patients in the past ten days."

"He's a cardiologist. He's going to lose a few patients."

"It hits him hard." Concern laced her tone. Libba, my I'll-never-settle-down friend, was in love.

Charlie needed to know about the pills, but I doubted I'd convince Libba to tell him when she was strung out on diet pills and insomnia. "Do you want to go swimming?"

She stared at me like I was the crazy woman in the room. "Swimming? It's not even six."

"Yet you're in my kitchen. I swim laps in the morning. If you're up and here, you might as well come with me. I'll loan you a suit."

She gave a put-upon sigh. "Fine."

I tilted my head. "Wait. I thought Charlie's kids liked you. That whole crazy eights marathon." We'd had a few interminable days of rain, and Libba had entertained Charlie's children.

"I thought they did, too. But something changed. I can't figure out what I did. Maybe Olivia put them up to it."

"Olivia?"

"Charlie's ex-wife."

"Ah." No woman would want her ex-husband with Libba. My friend was gorgeous and wild and great fun. She hopped on planes on the spur of the moment. Paris for a concert? Why not? There's a bull fight in Madrid? Let's go! She dressed with effort-less elegance. Sexy. Chic. Never demure. And the husky rasp of her voice brought grown men to their knees. "How long until they leave for camp?"

"Two very long weeks."

"Remind me of their names."

"Laine and CJ. They're twins."

"How old?"

"Twelve."

"Old enough to know better than to meddle with medication."

She lifted a brow and stretched her long, tanned legs.

"Supposing they'd messed with heart or diabetes medication?"

"I don't have those."

"You need to tell Charlie."

"Which will make them hate me more."

"They'll get over it."

"Fine," she ceded. "But not today. I'll tell him when we can manage some time alone." Then she pressed her hands together as if in prayer, and hope lit her tired eyes. "Can Grace watch them this weekend?"

"We're going to the farm."

Her face fell.

"You could come with us." I suggested.

She snorted. "To do what? I doubt being hot and buggy will improve their temperaments."

Or hers. Libba could ride and shoot, but she preferred her outdoor time close to a pool. Preferably a pool with a staff available to bring her drinks.

She steepled her fingers and served up her most winning smile. "Maybe you could take the kids!"

"Charlie might object. I imagine he wants to see his children. Also, you just said hot and buggy would make them more unpleasant."

"Two more weeks. Two more weeks." Libba's new mantra.

"Wait here." I hurried upstairs, threw on a swimsuit, grabbed an extra for Libba, and returned to the kitchen, where I nodded toward the back door. "Let's swim. By the time we get back, Aggie will be here. She'll fix breakfast."

"Pancakes?"

"If that's what you want." Aggie worked magic in the kitchen. Perfect, golden-brown pancakes were no challenge for her.

We drove my TR6 to the club. With the top down, the wind teased strands of hair from my ponytail and tugged at the collar of my shirt.

"I'm surprised you still swim in the mornings," said Libba.

"Why?"

"You did find a body in the pool."

"True." I shuddered. "But think of all the times I went swimming without touching a corpse."

"I suppose you're right. Although, if there is a body in the pool. I'll never forgive you."

I was fairly certain that finding Madeline's body floating in the deep end was a singular occurrence. If it wasn't, I needed to examine my life choices. I parked, and we walked to the pool, where I shrugged off Anarchy's shirt, kicked my shoes under a chaise, and dove in.

"Did you see *Deep Red*?" Libba sat on the pool's edge and let her lower legs accustom to the cool water. "It's a horror movie. Actually, kind of silly, but there was a doll..." she rubbed a palm across her mouth.

"A doll?" I prompted.

"Scared the living daylights out of me. I've never liked dolls, but this one—" she crossed her arms over her chest and shuddered "—it was terrifying."

Where was she going with this?

"Charlie teased me about it."

"About what?"

"My pediophobia. It's a fear of dolls."

"Since when are you afraid of dolls?"

"Since forever. Not Raggedy Ann. But the china dolls that blink? You better believe it. At any rate, the kids must have heard Charlie teasing me. They put a creepy doll in my bed."

"How terrifying," I deadpanned.

"Don't be so blasé. I know how you reacted to a rubber snake in your bed."

"Snakes slither and hiss and have fangs and venom."

"Not rubber snakes."

"I didn't know the snake was rubber. Besides, snakes are alive. Dolls are inanimate objects."

"That frighten me."

Throwing stones at her irrational fear when the word "copperhead" sent my heart racing wasn't fair. "You're right. I'm sorry. What did you do?"

"Screamed. Loud enough that the Bondurants heard me and came running." The Bondurants lived across the hall from Libba. They were pushing eighty, walked in Loose Park every day (while holding hands), and were the cutest couple I'd ever met.

"And?"

"Hal took care of it for me. But I was so discombobulated I didn't pay attention when I took my sleeping pills. That doll, it was old-fashioned. You know the kind. Porcelain face. Glass eyes." She shuddered deeply. "Silky hair. Frilly dress."

None of which sounded remotely scary.

"They put a knife in her hand."

I locked my jaw and sealed my lips to keep the laughter at bay.

Rather than risk Libba's ire (the temptation to tease was nearly insurmountable), I sank beneath the surface and swam. My arms and legs cut through the water. Lap after lap, my body answered the call to movement, and my brain tried to settle. Usually swimming gave me clarity. I needed clarity. Especially for Beau. But with Libba sitting on the side of the pool, her impatience evident with each flip of each page of last month's *Cosmo*, clarity proved elusive.

The blackbirds that appeared each season as soon as the first French fry hit the pool deck swooped, and Libba covered her head as if she were a character in *The Birds*. "Are you done yet?"

Bringing her had been a mistake.

"Five more laps."

She huffed and flapped her magazine at the too-bold birds.

When I emerged from the water, she handed me a towel. "Let's go." She'd waited patiently (not so patiently) and wanted the promised pancakes.

Together, we walked back to my car.

"You do this every morning?" Libba, who'd managed ten slow laps, leaned her wet head against the back of the passenger's seat.

I slipped the key into the ignition. "I do." I used to swim earlier, in the dark. Those days were over.

"And you're not exhausted? You must have swum a thousand laps."

"Not even close." I turned on the engine and put the car in gear.

We sped down the club's winding drive and Libba fiddled with the radio, stopping when Jessi Colter sang *I'm not Lisa*.

"You like this song?" I asked, mildly surprised.

"Let's just say I can relate."

"Charlie has a thing for his ex-wife?"

She snorted. "No. But his kids do."

"She is their mother."

She lowered her sunglasses and glared at me over the rims. "Whose side are you on?"

"Yours. But—"

"No buts."

I stopped for a red light at Ward Parkway and took the opportunity to study my friend. "Do you love Charlie?"

She crossed her arms over her chest and stared through the windshield.

"Do you?" I insisted.

"Yes." Her admission was grudging. She totally loved him.

"And he loves his kids."

"The light is green."

I pressed the accelerator.

"What's your point, Ellison?"

I cut through my still sleepy neighborhood. "Find a way to be something other than a mother. Show them how much fun you are. Show them you care about them." Good advice. I should follow it with Beau. I turned right and slammed on the brakes.

Libba, who wasn't wearing a seatbelt, caught herself on the dash. "What the hell?" Her outraged gaze shifted from me to the woman standing in front of the car.

Joanne Woodfield stood in the street wearing a nightgown. Her hair was a mess. Her eyes were wide. And I wasn't sure she actually saw us. Either she was on drugs or in shock, and I couldn't imagine Joanne taking drugs.

Had I hit her? I didn't think so. I threw the car in park and hurried to her side. "Are you hurt?"

"Help. I need your help." Then she ran toward her house.

Libba and I gaped at the brick colonial and Joanne's retreating back, then we followed her. We passed through the open front door and stopped in the front hall. The empty front hall. Joanne had disappeared.

"I have a bad feeling about this," said Libba.

That made two of us. "Joanne?" I called.

"Upstairs." Joanne's hysterical tone did not make me want to climb the stairs. "Hurry!"

"Do we have to?" Libba whispered.

"You can stay here." I didn't mean it.

"Great. I'll make coffee. She looks like she needs it." Libba had ignored my sarcasm and latched onto my suggestion.

Before I could argue or point out her cowardice, she disappeared down a hallway.

Alone, I climbed the stairs. "Joanne?"

Her sobs pulled me forward. I stepped through the door to the master bedroom, already sure of what I'd find—Joanne huddled above Lee's unmoving body.

CHAPTER FOUR

D id entering the bedroom with Joanne and spotting Lee on the floor count as finding a body? Surely not. I'd followed a hysterical woman upstairs. I'd hoped to offer help I wasn't qualified to give. It wasn't like I'd tripped over a body in the dark or run over a corpse. I hadn't found Lee.

Who was I kidding? For Mother, entering a room where a dead man lay on the floor would count. Already, I heard her scolding in my head. *Ellison, must you find bodies? People are talking, and I don't like what they're saying.*

I swallowed, and the click of my suddenly parched throat was outrageously loud.

Loud enough for Joanne to glance over her shoulder and stare at me as if she wondered why I was still lingering in the doorway.

I took a tiny step forward.

"The ambulance is coming," she told her husband. "Ellison is here."

Not that I could do anything helpful. Libba making coffee was more useful than my hovering just inside the door.

"Can't you do anything for him?" she demanded. As if she

believed I possessed useful skills. Skills I'd successfully kept hidden for decades.

I had no skills, and Lee was beyond help. I'd seen that gray pallor too often to offer her false hope. What could I do for Joanne? I crouched next to her on the floor and rested my hand on her shoulder. "Who can I call?"

"No!" She ground the heels of her hands into her wet eyes. "He's not gone. He's not."

Joanne and Lee had adult children. "Should I call your daughter?"

She shook off my hand and glared at me. "He's not gone. He's resting."

"Of course he is." I placated with the best of them. "But your daughter might want to—"

"No, Ellison! Lee will be fine."

Denial wasn't just a river in Egypt.

"I'm so sorry." Joanne raked her fingers through her messy hair, and her red-rimmed gaze returned to her husband's body. "I shouldn't snap at you. But there's no need to worry anyone else. Lee will be fine. Dr. Ardmore said his heart condition was minor. A few lifestyle changes—control his blood pressure, less salt, cut back on red meat, limit the martinis, exercise regularly, give up cigars."

"Charlie is his doctor?" Maybe I could help.

Joanne nodded.

I left her, hurried to the top of the stairs, and bellowed, "Libba!"

She appeared in the foyer with a familiar red can in her hands. "What?"

"Call Charlie."

Her eyes narrowed. At my words or my tone? Thankfully, she'd didn't argue. Instead, she gave a curt nod. "On it."

"Tell him to hurry." With leaden feet, I returned to Joanne. And Lee.

"Did you call Charlie Ardrmore? Is he coming?" Desperation had a voice.

"Libba's calling him now." I ducked into Joanne's bathroom, grabbed a handful of tissues, and took them to her.

Joanne mopped her eyes and blew her nose with her left hand. Her right kept a bruising grip on her husband's lifeless fingers. "Lee Woodfield, open your eyes." Anger laced her tone, as if Lee's possum act was designed to annoy her.

Lee didn't respond.

"Damnit, Lee. Listen to me. Open your eyes."

Lee's lids remained firmly closed, and a sob rose from Joanne's chest. "You can't leave me. I can't do this without you."

I was an intruder on her grief. I fidgeted with the damp collar of Anarchy's shirt.

"Open your eyes, and I swear I'll never complain about your dirty socks on the floor ever again." Joanne held herself still, as if the smallest movement might keep Lee from opening his eyelids. "I'll let you sleep in on Saturday mornings. I won't say a word when you eat a third strip of bacon."

"I can call my husband," I offered. "Anarchy might be able to help."

"Does he know CPR?" An actual skill. One I ought to perfect.

"I'm sure he does." And I was sure Lee was beyond CPR.

"Call him."

I crossed to the phone next to the bed and dialed home.

"Jones' residence." Aggie sounded sunny. I pictured her smile and her wild muumuu and her oversized hoop earrings, and I desperately wished to be home.

"Aggie, it's me." My voice was surprisingly steady. "I need to speak with Anarchy."

"He's on his way to the station. He just walked out the door."

"Please, try to catch him. It's important. An emergency."

"Of course."

I waited with the receiver pressed to my ear and prayed Aggie caught Anarchy in time.

"Ellison?" Concern sharpened my name on Anarchy's lips. "I thought you went swimming. What's wrong?"

"I'm at the Woodfields' house. We need you."

"You didn't go swimming?"

"I did. Then, on the way home, Joanne ran into the street." How long had we been here? Where was the ambulance? "Lee had a heart attack."

"What's the address?"

"Our street. Drive toward the park. The next block. The second home from the corner. I parked the car in front of their house."

"On my way."

I returned the receiver to its cradle.

Hopefully, Charlie was also en route.

Next to Lee, Joanne was rocking as fresh tears streamed down her cheeks. "Ellison?"

"Yes."

"He's not answering me."

And he wouldn't. Not ever again. Poor Joanne.

"You'd better call my daughter. My address book is in the desk in the kitchen."

I moved toward the door. "Can I get you anything?"

She scowled at me, as if offering coffee or brandy or a glass of water was insensitive. "No."

I descended to the kitchen and accepted a cup of coffee from Libba, who asked, "Lee?"

"He's gone."

"And you left her? To get coffee?" She nodded at the cup she'd given me.

"No." The coffee was just a bonus. I opened Joanne's desk drawer and sifted through its contents—a box of unused checks, used check registers, bank statements held together with a rubber band, scissors, tape, paper clips, the country club directory. Where was her address book?

"What are you doing?" Libba asked

"She wants me to call her daughter."

Libba paled. "Tracy? You're sure he's gone? Charlie's on his way."

"So is Anarchy." Was it awful that I couldn't wait to hand over the whole tragic situation to a doctor and a police detective? Probably. "Maybe I should take Joanne some coffee."

"Not everyone needs coffee as much as you do."

A, that was just ridiculous. B, she made me sound like an addict. I said as much. Where was the address book? I shifted a sheaf of letters.

"If the shoe fits."

Better coffee than pitchers of gin martinis or diet pills.

"The first step is admitting you have a problem." Libba smirked at me as if she held some sort of moral high ground. She didn't. And her attitude was supremely annoying.

I gave up my search to glare at her. "People who live in glass houses."

"I don't drink much coffee."

No. She drank martinis. By the gallon. And took diet pills. And, until recently, she'd run through men like tissues. "There are other addictions, Libba."

She donned her you're-in-for-it-now expression—left brow lowered, right brow lifted, flattened lips, and her chin to her chest—and I readied myself for a sharp retort.

The doorbell rang, saving us from a spat.

We practically fell over ourselves, hurrying to the front of the house

Anarchy and Charlie waited on the stoop.

"Lee's upstairs," I told them.

Charlie pounded up the front stairs, and Libba trailed behind him.

Anarchy lingered, wrapping me in his arms. "Are you okay?"

"Better now that you're here." I melted into his embrace, resting my head against his shoulder and drawing my first deep breath since seeing Lee's body.

Anarchy's gentle fingers tilted my head upward, and his gaze searched my face. "You're sure?"

"I'm sure."

He kissed me, too quickly, then followed Charlie upstairs.

The bell rang again, and I pulled open the front door.

"You called for an ambulance?" The man, who was in his twenties, had serious eyes and ridiculous sideburns. He looked like a character from *Emergency*.

"Upstairs," I told him. "Master bedroom."

He swept past me.

I trudged after him, pausing in the bedroom doorway so I wouldn't be in the way. The men huddled around Lee. Maybe I'd made a mistake. Maybe there was hope. I crossed my fingers.

Anarchy caught my eye and gave a small, sad shake of his head.

I'd been right. Lee was gone.

"Ellison," he said. "Would you please take Joanne downstairs?"

"Of course."

Anarchy led the shaking woman to me, and I wrapped my arm around her waist. "Let's get you some coffee."

"I can't leave him. I can't."

"We'll take good care of him," Anarchy promised.

She drooped, and only my arm at her waist kept her from sinking to the floor.

"Joanne, you need to be strong. I'm sure your husband would want you to be strong." Anarchy's voice was gentle.

Joanne nodded, and I took her to the kitchen, where Libba poured her a mug.

Joanne wrapped her fingers around the cup as if the warm porcelain was her tether to sanity.

I helped her into her desk chair. "Where's your book, Joanne? I haven't yet called your daughter."

"I'll do it." She reached for the phone and dialed. "Tracy, it's Mom. Your dad—" her voice broke. "Your dad—" she pressed her palm against her lips and held out the receiver. To me.

I took the phone. I'd have rather accepted a snake. "Tracy, this is Ellison Jones. I'm with your mom."

"What happened to Dad?"

A heart attack? "Dr. Ardmore is with him now."

"You're at the hospital?"

"Your parents' home."

Her swallow was audible. "Tell Mom I love her. I'm on my way."

I hung up.

"Is she coming?" Joanne sounded completely shattered, as if the pieces of her life had been ground to dust.

"She's on her way. She asked me to tell you she loves you."

Joanne's face crumpled like a used tissue. "She said that? Really?"

She was surprised her daughter loved her? My hand trembled as I clumsily patted her back. "She did."

Libba rolled her eyes at my ineffectual attempt at comfort.

I didn't see her doing more than leaning against Joanne's counter.

A thump came from upstairs, and Joanne's back tightened, her head disappearing between her shoulders like a turtle.

How could we help her? Her cup was nearly full, but coffee meant comfort to me. And, I had nothing else to offer. "May I warm your cup?"

"No, thank you. It will upset my stomach."

"Something stronger?" asked Libba.

"It's not yet eight in the morning. I can't." Seven-thirty was too early for a drink. Unquestionably. But the circumstances were appalling, and Joanne sounded as if she wanted someone to convince her.

"A brandy might help." Libba, ever the devil on one's shoulder.

"No." Joanne nodded as if she desperately wanted a glass. "I can't."

"A wee nip? It's medicinal." From her devilish perch, Libba led Joanne to the dark side.

Joanne eyed the clock on the wall, then winced. "I can't."

I cast a desperate look at Libba. What could we say? Do? "You're sure you don't want more coffee?" We could even add a dash of whiskey to her mug. Oh dear Lord. Now who was the temptress? At least I hadn't said the words aloud.

"Mom? Where are you?" Tracy's voice rang through the house.

I drew a relieved breath and called, "We're in the kitchen."

Tracy rushed into the room. Her pretty face was free of make-up, and she'd scraped her hair into a messy ponytail. She wore a faded madras housecoat and dime store flip-flops. Her face was flushed, as if she'd sprinted to her parents' home. Spotting her mother, she rushed to Joanne's side and crouched next to her. "Mom?"

Joanne stared at her hands in her lap, as if facing her daughter was painful. "They're still upstairs with your father."

"Is he...?"

A tear splashed against Joanne's laced fingers.

"Mom?"

Joanne gnawed at her lower lip.

When her mother didn't answer, Tracy looked at me.

Why me? "Dr. Ardmore and the EMTs are with your dad."

"And Anarchy," Libba added.

Tracy frowned. "Anarchy?"

KILLING ME SOFTLY   43

"My husband," I explained. "We live down the street." With any luck, Tracy didn't know what Anarchy did for a living.

Her forehead creased. Her lips flattened. Her red cheeks paled. She stood, and her hands gripped the top rung of her mother's ladder-back desk chair. "Your husband is a homicide detective."

So much for luck. I gave a tiny nod.

Tracy swayed. "Was Dad murdered?"

"Of course not. No one would hurt your father." Joanne lifted her head and glared. "Besides, murder?" Her face tightened with distaste. "That sort of thing doesn't happen to our kind of people. Your father is having an incident with his heart. That is all." Joanne's family was too prominent for Lee to be murdered. The mere suggestion of foul play was enough to rouse her from her misery.

Because her husband was not having an incident with his heart, because he was dead, because her world was about to implode, I didn't argue. The truth? Social position, an impressive education, a revered family name—they didn't really keep the wolf from the door. Murder could tap anyone with its bony finger.

"It's just a heart attack." Joanne's hands were clenched so tightly together that her knuckles whitened.

Tracy closed her eyes, tilted her head toward the ceiling, and gave an audible sigh.

"Don't take that tone with me," Joanne snapped.

"Mom, I didn't say anything."

"You didn't have to."

"Just tell me what happened to Dad."

"He had a heart attack."

"Major or minor? A few more details? Please?"

Joanne sat straighter in her chair and scowled at everyone in the kitchen. "It was a normal morning. I got up early. Your father lingered in bed, just like he always does. I told him the time.

Nicely. He grumbled, as usual. Then he dragged himself out of bed and took a shower. Meanwhile, I stripped the sheets and tidied our bedroom."

"Mom." Tracy didn't need a play-by- play of every second of Joanne's morning.

Neither did I.

"He came out of the bathroom, and I asked if he took his pills. He forgets. Every single day. I remind him every day. Every single day."

"Mom."

"Fine. Your father took his pills and got dressed while I collected his dirty towels. Today is the day I wash whites."

"I know, Mom. What happened to Dad?"

"When I finished in the bathroom, he was on the bedroom floor. Not moving. I called an ambulance, then ran outside to get help. Ellison nearly hit me."

"You ran into the street like you'd never heard of traffic." For all her faults, Libba was always in my corner. "You're lucky Ellison is a good driver."

Joanne huffed, and I suspected if she felt better, she'd argue the point.

"Your mother was distraught," I told Tracy. "We came inside with her and called Dr. Ardmore."

She pressed her palms to her cheeks. "A major heart attack." She shifted her gaze to me. "And your husband? If Dad wasn't murdered, why is he here?"

Because dealing with a body and Joanne's raw emotions had been too much for me. Because Joanne had demanded answers I didn't want to give. Because Anarchy was my rock. "He's certi- fied in CPR."

Tracy nodded, as if my answer made perfect sense. Then she shuffled to the kitchen table, where she sank onto the closest chair. "Not murder," she murmured. "A heart attack."

"That's what I told you." Anguish and annoyance battled for supremacy in Joanne's voice.

Maybe the past year, one in which I'd found multiple murder victims, was catching up with me. Maybe I saw evil where none existed. But something niggled at me. I shifted my gaze from the dead man's worried daughter to his grief-stricken wife. Was Joanne acting? Had she killed her husband?

Her sorrow and devastation seemed real.

But I'd been fooled before.

CHAPTER FIVE

Platte County, which was immediately to the north of Kansas City, was filled with rolling hills, gorgeous vistas, fresh air, and sunshine.

Grace, who sat in the back seat with a silent Beau, asked. "How much farther?"

I twisted in my seat to stare at her. "You've been to the farm a hundred times."

"It's not like I pay attention."

"Fifteen minutes," I supplied.

She sighed. Deeply.

"What?"

"I need a bathroom."

"Seriously? Can't you hold it?"

Beau snickered. That tiny sound counted as progress, the first hint of levity I'd heard from him in days.

"Nooooooo." My daughter was nothing if not dramatic. "I need a bathroom now."

"Look around." A smidge of frustration elbowed its way into my tone. "Do you see a service station? You can hold it, or you can squat at the side of the road."

That got a giggle from Beau.

"Anarchy, tell her we need to stop. Please."

"Where, Grace? We're surrounded by pastures."

She huffed at Anarchy's unhelpful reply.

Another louder giggle from the peanut gallery.

My lips quirked and the tightness around my heart loosened.

"Drive faster," Grace begged.

"I'm driving the speed limit."

"Anarchy," Grace whined. "Please? There's not another car for miles."

"I'm a cop, Grace. I can't speed."

I secretly suspected that Anarchy's rule following had more to do with his personality than his profession.

"I have to tinkle." Grace tapped her foot rapidly.

Beau laughed.

And I wondered if Grace even needed a bathroom.

Anarchy's knowing smirk said he'd figured out her game long before I did. "Maybe a song will take your mind off your bladder."

"The radio only gets country stations."

"We'll sing." Anarchy tapped a beat against the steering wheel with his wedding ring. "Ninety-nine bottles of beer on the wall, ninety-nine bottles of beer." My husband possessed a good singing voice.

From the back seat, Beau joined him. "Take one down, pass it around—"

"You two are not funny."

Again, Beau laughed.

If singing about liquid when Grace needed a bathroom made Beau laugh, I was in. "Ninety-eight bottles of beer on the wall."

I felt the weight of Grace's scowl on the back of my neck.

Finn, who rode in the way back with Max, howled.

"He doesn't like your singing," said Beau.

"Apparently not."

"The dog has taste," Grace sniped.

"I know how you feel about my singing. There's no need to rub it in."

Beau snickered, and I hid a smile.

"Anarchy, has Mom told you about the farm?"

The chorus on Anarchy's lips faded. "Not much."

"It belonged to my grandparents."

"They were farmers?"

"Weekend farmers. They leased the fields and the pastures to locals and kept about thirty acres for themselves. There's a creek and a pond and my grandmother's vegetable garden."

"And the woods," Grace added. She'd magically forgotten her urgent need for a bathroom.

"And the woods," I agreed. "There's also a barn and a pasture for the horses, the house, and a hunting cabin. The Smiths take care of the property. Mr. Smith deals with the tenants and the horses and maintains the hunting blinds. His wife takes care of the house and garden."

"How often do your parents visit?"

"Rarely. Mother doesn't like the country." Mother didn't like bugs, dust, the drone of locusts, cistern plumbing, gravel roads, snakes (I agreed with her about that), rodents, the lack of morning paper delivery, or being lazy. The charms of a shady hammock and a good book were lost on her. Mother's perfect day included bridge at the club, running a committee meeting or two, bossing her household staff and daughters, and cocktails at five. "Take the next right."

The turn signal clicked loudly inside the car.

"We're the only car on the road," said Grace. "You can go a little faster."

"It's the law," Anarchy replied.

I didn't need to turn my head to know she'd rolled her eyes.

A small heart-warming snicker from her cohort in the backseat confirmed it.

A plume of dust followed our rented station wagon down the drive to the farmhouse.

Anarchy parked the car in front of the house and stared. "You've been holding out on me."

"What do you mean?"

"This place is incredible." He stared at the enormous, red-brick, Victorian farmhouse with the wrap-around porch that my grandparents had built. "How old is it?"

"Around eighteen-ninety," Grace replied. "And it has the plumbing to prove it."

"Grace!"

"What? It's true. Speaking of—" she opened the car door and raced toward the house.

"I guess she did have to go. Horses or creek?" I asked Beau.

"Horses." Beau had more enthusiasm in his voice than I'd heard in days.

"How does Finn do with horses?"

"I don't know."

"Wait for Grace to come back, then leave the dogs with us."

When Grace returned, she claimed Beau's hand, and the twosome scampered off to the pasture.

I got out of the car, stretched, then opened the tailgate.

Max and Finn jumped out, shook as if their lives depended on it, then took off after the kids.

"No!"

They ignored me, running straight to the fence where Grace and Beau perched on the lowest rail and called to the horses.

"Grace!"

She turned, leapt to the ground, and caught Finn's collar.

Easy, since Finn seemed frozen, his gaze fixed on the ambling horses. With Grace's fingers wrapped around his collar, the dog sat on his haunches.

Anarchy claimed my hand, and we walked toward our family.

"Everything okay?" I asked.

"Why do you ask?"

"You were very quiet on the drive up here. Aside from the singing." That had been loud.

"I was thinking." He rubbed his free hand across his chin.

"About?"

He paused, and I stared up at his lean face. The late-afternoon sun kissed his hair, gilding each strand. His lips twisted into a wry smile.

"What?" I asked.

"How well do you know Joanne Woodfield?"

The iced coffee I'd sipped on our drive north soured in my stomach. "Why do you ask?"

"There have been three unexpected deaths in the past ten days."

The sourness in my stomach rose to my throat. Had Joanne killed Lee? "Are you saying those deaths were murders?"

"No." He took off his aviator sunglasses and looked into my eyes. "But did Joanne have any reason to kill her husband?"

"Not that I know of."

"But you could find out?"

I nodded. Slowly. Asking if a recent widow wanted her husband dead was horrible and gauche and not unheard of. "I'll keep my ears open. I imagine the funeral will be next week."

"You're going?"

"Of course. You should, too."

"Homicide detectives aren't always welcome at funerals."

"You're my husband."

"And a cop." He leaned forward and kissed the tip of my nose. "You might overlook the cop part. No one else does."

"Has someone been rude?"

"No. But I'm not a doctor or lawyer or CEO."

He was kind, steadfast, sexy, smart, and sexy (worth mentioning twice). He made me feel seen and appreciated like never before. He made my heart skip every time he looked into my eyes. He was worth a million lawyers or doctors or scions.

"I worry you'll come to your senses."

"Me?" Anarchy was the one who'd married a widowed, single mother, who found bodies nearly every time she left her house. "I'm the lucky one."

His smile was dazzling. There wasn't a woman on earth who wouldn't melt into a pile of goo upon seeing that smile.

Unable to form actual words, I pushed a strand of hair away from my face, stalling until my vocal cords could manage speech.,

A sharp bark claimed my attention, dragging my gaze from Anarchy's coffee brown eyes. "We need to police Finn."

He nodded, and we joined the kids and dogs at the fence.

Woof!

Finn had regained his faculties.

Woof!

The horses flicked their ears and ignored him. He danced on his paws as if he'd just met super-sized playmates.

"Hush, Finn." He went down on his front legs and his stubby tail wagged so hard his butt shook.

Max suspended his search for small prey to stare at his over-eager friend.

"Grace, grab a halter for King." The sorrel gelding had a calm nature. He was the best choice to meet Finn.

She nodded and disappeared into the barn, emerging a moment later with a faded blue halter and lead rope.

King ambled toward us, and Grace climbed the fence and approached him in the pasture. She rubbed the blaze on his nose, and he gave her an affectionate nudge.

Grace slipped the halter over his ears, fastened the buckle, and led the gelding to the gate.

"That's King," I told Beau. "When we go riding, he'll be your horse."

Beau's eyes widened. "He's really big."

"And really gentle. You'll love him, and he'll love you."

Beau did not look convinced. Twin furrows bracketed the area between his brows.

Oh dear Lord. The last thing I wanted was to add to his worries.

Next to us, Finn whined his excitement.

"Finn, calm down." My voice was too sharp, but Finn didn't care. He waggled his body, flopped onto the grass, then rolled over, showing King his belly.

The horse looked amused.

"Ellison!"

I turned and saw Mrs. Smith hurrying toward us.

"There's a phone call for you."

I winced. "Mother?" Already? We'd been gone less than three hours.

"No. Libba."

I frowned.

"She said it was urgent that she speak with you."

I glanced at Beau and the dog and the horse.

"We've got this covered, Mom." Grace pursed her lips at my useless, and apparently evident, worry.

"You're sure?"

My daughter rolled her eyes, but my husband offered a reassuring smile. "I'll stay with them."

THE TELEPHONE RESTED ON A TABLE FROM THE 1940s. SOLID. Ugly. Its aged wood marked with countless glass rings.

I picked up the receiver, dialed Libba's number, sank onto a faded, comfortable, if-Mother-ever-came-to-the-farm-and-saw-the-thin-fabric-on-its-arms-she'd-have-it-recovered-or-replaced-in-a-New-York minute couch, and stared at a painting of a black labrador with a limp duck in its mouth.

"Hello." Libba's pitch was too high.

"It's me."

"Took you long enough."

"I just got your message. What's wrong?"

"Is Anarchy investigating Charlie?"

"What?"

"That's not a no."

"No. Anarchy is not investigating Charlie."

"The police? Are they investigating? What about Anarchy's partner? Peters?"

"Libba, what's happened?"

"I saw Prudence Dawes at the club. She suggested Owen's and Lee's deaths are Charlie's fault. That they were intentional."

"Since when do you let anything Prudence says upset you?" Prudence was a jealous, mean, horse-toothed shrew, who had an affair with my late husband.

"Prudence repeats whatever she hears. That means other people are talking."

"It's ridiculous. Charlie is not murdering his patients."

"I know," she snapped. "But it looks terrible—healthy men dying like this."

"People die. Otherwise healthy men have heart attacks. Women, too. It's not Charlie's fault."

"Try explaining that at the bridge table. Especially when people whisper rather than speak openly about their concerns."

"Call Mother."

"What?" Her voice reached a pitch best heard by dogs.

"Call her. She can squash rumors. Plus, she's on the hospital board." Mother was the chairman, and she'd been instrumental in bringing Charlie back to Kansas City. "She won't stand for anyone maligning Charlie."

"Can you call her?"

"It'll mean more coming from you."

"You're her daughter."

"Which is why she poo-poos my opinions."

"She's terrifying."

"Use that to Charlie's advantage."

"You won't call her?"

"I'm away for the weekend."

"Fine." She huffed, as if she were doing me an enormous favor. "When will you be back?"

Did she plan on waiting till I could call Mother? "Late Sunday."

"Think about how we can prove Charlie's innocence."

"Libba, Charlie can't cause a heart attack."

"You're right." She sighed. Deeply. I'd better call Frances. Goodbye."

I returned the receiver to the cradle and took a deep, cleansing breath. Libba was my best friend, but sometimes her penchant for drama exhausted me. I wouldn't say no to a few weeks without drama. Or dead bodies.

Brnng, brnng.

I stared at the phone.

"Ellison, would you please get that?" Mrs. Smith's voice carried from the kitchen. "I'm kneading bread dough."

I picked up the receiver. "Hello."

"I'm calling for Ellison Russell."

"Jones."

"Pardon me?"

"It's Ellison Jones. And, this is she."

"Ellison? It's Jane Addison."

I sank back onto the couch. If Jane was calling me, if she'd taken the time to track down this phone number, there was a problem. Another problem.

"What can I do for you, Jane?" "

"Have you talked to Karma recently?"

"Not in the past day or two. She's due to arrive in Kansas City on Monday."

"Do you have a number for her?"

"Not with me. Did you find a house for her?"

"No," the realtor snapped.

"Jane." Asking was a mistake, but I did it anyway. "What's wrong?"

"You haven't talked to her?"

"I already told you I haven't."

"She didn't call and tell you about the Gilman's place?"

The Gilman's. I pictured the house—a brick colonial with a circle drive and a large backyard. "The kitchen is a redo." Ann Gilman didn't need a kitchen. The woman cooked less than I did.

"That's not the point. Karma bought a house. Without me."

There it was. Jane had missed out on a fat commission. "I don't know anything about that."

"Hmph. Is it true you found Lee Woodfield's body?"

I blinked at the sudden change of topic. "His wife found him."

"But you were there?" she insisted.

"I didn't find him."

"Will Joanne stay in that house?" Pure Jane. She never let a little thing like grief get in the way of a listing.

"I'm sure I don't know." Joanne's husband had been dead less than forty-eight hours. Seriously?

"What about Elaine Sandingham?"

"You'd have to speak with her family."

"I could get them top dollar."

"I know nothing about their plans, Jane."

"You could ask." Annoyance bled into her tone.

"So could you." My tone matched hers.

"Maybe I should get a list of Charlie Ardmore's patients. They're dropping like flies."

"What a terrible thing to say." And exactly what Libba worried about. "I'd be careful Jane."

"Of what?"

"To suggest that Charlie's patients die when they shouldn't is almost libelous."

"Is that what I said?"

"It's what you hinted."

"Look at the facts, Ellison. Three patients in the last ten days."

My eye twitched. Not a brief twitch. No, this twitch reverberated across my face and clear down my stiffened spine. "Jane, I don't like what you're suggesting. Those three patients had heart conditions."

"Mild heart conditions. You're neighbors with Charlie. Ask him."

"Charlie doesn't discuss his patients with me."

"Well, his patients are discussing him."

"Charlie is not responsible for their deaths. And you're flirting with libel."

"I'm only reporting what others are saying. Besides, no one is saying he's a killer. They're just realizing he may not be the hot-shot doctor they first believed him to be."

The gossip Jane was eagerly peddling could ruin Charlie's practice.

"He is a hot-shot doctor."

"If you say so." She used a placating tone, one usually reserved for mothers who hoped, prayed, made deals with deities that appeasing a toddler would stall a gathering tantrum.

"I say so." My palms rubbed the back of my neck where tension shot both ways—down into my shoulders and up into skull.

"Oh, Ellison, relax. Death is good for realtors. About your sister—"

"What about her?" My patience with Janes was nearing its end.

"She doesn't need that enormous house. Not when it's just her. I can find her something much better."

"Undoubtedly."

Jane ignored the dryness of my tone. "How could she do this to me? She has some realtor friend in California, who's friends with Hal Robinson, the listing agent for the Gilmans. They cut me out, and your sister let them."

Oh dear Lord. I didn't have the time or energy for this conversation.

"She bought the place sight unseen."

"Karma is familiar with the neighborhood."

"There's more to real estate than the neighborhood."

"Really? I always thought it was location, location, location."

"Unless the place is a money pit." Did Jane know something about the Gilman's house? Had Karma made a mistake? More likely, it was sour grapes over a lost commission. "That house needs more than a kitchen redo. The whole place needs a refresh."

A refresh we could handle.

"Have you heard anything about the Dixons' house?" I asked.

My question surprised us both, and Jane was quiet for long seconds. "No. What do you know about the Rileys' house?"

"The Rileys?" Beau's parents' house. Jane had no shame. "Jane, I'm here for time with my family. I need to let you go."

"The Riley boy is with you?"

"Yes."

"Is his father selling that house?"

"I honestly don't know."

"What will you do about Karma?"

"I realize you're disappointed in missing out on a sale, but—"

"I'm close to earning the chairman's award this month.

Helping your sister find a house would have put me firmly in the lead."

"Hopefully you'll find another client, another sale."

"Karma would have guaranteed me that award."

"I'm sorry, Jane. There's nothing I can do."

"But—"

"And I really do need to go. We can talk when I'm back in town." I eased the receiver toward its cradle.

"But, Ellison—"

"Have a nice weekend. Bye-bye." I hung up and stared at the labrador for long seconds. Were people really speculating about Charlie?

Had someone murdered those men?

I stood, suddenly desperate to discuss the whole mess with Anarchy.

CHAPTER SIX

"Ellison?"

I turned toward Mrs. Smith.

She wore her faded hair in a neat bun and a white apron over a soft blue shirtwaist dress. She couldn't look more different from Aggie, but the expression in her eyes was exactly the same. Curious. Kind. Intelligent. "Mr. Smith has a pork shoulder on the smoker, and I made baked beans."

"That sounds delicious." Much better than the cold-cut sandwiches I had planned. Slapping sliced turkey or ham, Swiss cheese, tomato slices, and mayo on a slice of bread represented the pinnacle of my culinary achievements. Safe to say, Anarchy had not married me for my cooking skills. "Thank you."

"You're welcome. It's a treat to have you and Grace here and to meet your new husband. Would Beau like my peach pie for dessert?"

"Everyone likes your peach pie."

A gentle smile curled her lips.

"Hasn't it won first place in the county fair three years running?"

Pink stained her cheeks. "Yes."

"Beau will love it."

"Does seven suit you for dinner?"

"We'll be ready." I slipped through the front door to the porch, and the dogs greeted me as if I were newly home from an extended trip around the world. Their stubby tails wagged hard enough to shake their doggy behinds, and they both wore enormous grins.

"Have you behaved?" I asked.

Woof! Finn replied.

Unsure if his bark meant yes or no, I scratched behind his ears.

His tail (and butt) wagged harder.

"Everything okay?" Anarchy rounded the corner of the house and studied me with worry-filled eyes. "You've been gone a long time."

I held up two fingers. "Two calls. Karma bought a house, not from Addison Jane."

The tension lining his handsome face eased. "Jane's not happy?"

"Understatement of the decade."

Finn nudged my hand for more scratches.

"She also hinted that Charlie is killing his patients."

"That's ridiculous."

"I agree. But the gossip won't do his practice any favors. Libba is worried."

"She was the second call?"

"Yes."

"Come with me." Anarchy claimed my hand.

"Where are we going?"

"I saw a hammock and I intend to laze in it with my wife."

"But Charlie—"

"Is in Kansas City. There's nothing we can do for him right now."

"Beau—"

"He and Grace have a couple of horses on long lines. Grace said they'd ride after they'd taken the edge off."

"Beau will ride King. Which horse is Grace riding?"

"She said you'd ask that." His lips quirked, and I was certain his eyes twinkled behind his sunglasses. "Sadie."

Sadie was a good-natured mare. She and Grace adored each other.

"That's all right." Still, a vision invaded my brain—Beau broken in an unmoving heap on the ground. "Maybe we should join them."

Anarchy's grasp on my hand tightened. "Hammock."

"But—"

"Ellison, you're acting as if he'll break. He senses your worry, and he tenses even more. Let him hang out with Grace. Trust him to be okay."

My shoulders sagged. "I'm doing it again. I'm making things worse for him."

"Not on purpose."

Guilt grabbed my throat tight enough to make my jaw ache. I blinked back tears.

"Oh, honey." Anarchy stopped on the path from the house to a stand of shade trees and wrapped his arms around my waist, pulling me close.

I rested my forehead against his chest and fought back a flood of tears.

"We're all muddling through."

"I need to do better than muddle."

"Because you need to be perfect?"

"No." Yes.

"You do realize perfection is impossible?"

"Beau deserves the best I can give him."

Anarchy's palm rubbed a gentle circle on my back. "Like you said at dinner, it's okay if he's not okay."

I felt his lips press against the top of my head, and the tight coil of worry that circled my heart loosened. "Hammock?"

He relaxed his hold on me and reclaimed my hand. "Hammock."

When we were swaying in the hammock, I said, "You seem to understand exactly how Beau is feeling,"

Anarchy shifted. "I do."

"How?"

The silence stretched.

Had I touched a nerve? "It's okay. You don't have to tell me."

"No. I want to. I never talk about this and I'm figuring out where to start.

I waited, not so patiently, for more.

"When I was twelve, my best friend was a guy named Paul Bishop. We played on the same sports teams, attended the same school, read the same comics, liked the same TV shows. We were inseparable."

I nestled closer. "Like Libba and me, but without sports or comics." Libba and I had bonded over our mother's fashion magazines, our love of shopping, and our deep antipathy toward mathematics.

His low chuckle reverberated through my chest, too. "Paul's dad was a professor like mine, and his mom stayed home. She drank."

I stiffened. I'd known when I asked, I might get a dark story.

"She picked us up from school one afternoon, and I could smell the liquor on her." He shifted his weight, and the hammock swayed. "I should have refused to get in the car, but I didn't want to cause a scene and embarrass my friend. She caused an accident."

"Paul?"

"He died."

"His mother?"

"She died, too. I nearly died." His hold on me tightened. "My mother knew Mrs. Bishop had a problem, but it was easier for her to share driving to school and little league practices with another mother. After the accident, she felt guilty. And I fell down a deep well of sadness. I was so sad I didn't care about climbing out of the well. And my mother hovered. She made things worse."

"How did you get better?"

"My dad took me to a psychologist. I wasn't just sad. I was angry. At Mrs. Bishop for the accident. At my mother for letting her drive us. At Paul for dying. At myself for not making a scene. I should have refused to get in the car. I should have made Paul stay with me."

I wanted to go back in time, wrap my arms around twelve-year-old Anarchy, and soothe his pain. But pain and grief and anger weren't that easily healed. If they were, I'd spend my days hugging Beau. "I hate that you went through that and I'm sorry you lost your friend."

"It was a long time ago."

Did we ever stop missing those we loved? A day might pass, a week, and then a smell or a sound or a song would remind us of the holes in our hearts. Time might heal, but it didn't erase, not those written indelibly on our hearts. I tilted my head and kissed his cheek. "I'm still sorry."

Anarchy's answering smile was a pebble that started a cascade. His smile tumbled through my heart, leaving me careening at the edge of overwhelming emotion. "I love you," I told him. I said it often, but if the past year had taught me nothing else, I'd learned that life could be fleeting. One should never miss the chance to say I love you.

"I am so damn lucky."

The hammock swayed. A bird twittered. A breeze made the late afternoon bearable.

"This is nice," Anarchy observed.

"Better than nice."

"We should come up here more often."

I hummed my agreement.

"I just need to avoid picking up so many cases."

"And I can avoid finding bodies." Although, finding bodies wasn't something one could avoid. It just happened. Over and over and over again. I snuggled closer. "Do you really think Lee's death is suspicious?"

Anarchy remained silent for long seconds. "Yes."

"And Owen's, too?"

"Possibly. Why?"

"Charlie didn't kill those men." I'd known Charlie my whole life. He wasn't a killer.

"Maybe he made a mistake with their medication."

"Hmph. It's possible, but Charlie's an excellent doctor."

"The other possibility is that their wives killed them."

"I'd believe one wife is capable of murder, but three?"

"The first two were natural, and Lee was murdered?"

"Joanne seemed bereft." Seemed was the operative word. "Maybe we're wrong. Maybe they all died of heart attacks." Anarchy rubbed his chest. "Possible, but I have a feeling."

I did too. One I wished I could ignore.

I woke up early and, without a nearby swimming pool, I contemplated staying in bed.

But the lemony light peeking through the curtains beckoned, and my fingers itched for the feel of charcoal on paper. I slid out from under the light quilt that covered our bed.

"Where are you going?" Anarchy mumbled.

"Coffee."

"I can get up," he offered.

With sleep softening his features, Anarchy was nearly irre-sistible. The temptation to return to bed nearly overwhelmed me, but I steeled my spine. "Don't. I'm going to sketch."

"You're sure?"

"Positive. Sleep." I descended to the kitchen, where Mrs. Smith, God bless her, had started a pot of coffee. I poured myself a cup and stepped onto the porch.

The morning air tasted sweet on my tongue, like fresh-cut clover. The light kissed all it touched with a golden promise. I sank into a rocking chair and warmed my fingers on the coffee mug.

"Can I sit with you?" The voice was small.

"Of course."

Beau took the chair next to mine, and Finn, who looked like he'd rather be sleeping, flopped in front of us.

"How are you this morning?" I asked.

"Fine."

I glanced at the boy whose feet barely touched the porch's painted planks. He wore a tee-shirt, shorts and scuffed sneakers. If he felt my gaze, he gave no sign. Instead, he picked at a scab on his knee.

"Pretty morning," I observed.

"I guess." He rubbed the toe of his sneaker against Finn's flank.

The sleepy dog looked up at his boy with adoring eyes.

"Are you hungry? Mrs. Smith makes a great breakfast."

"Not hungry."

And not in the mood to talk.

We sat in silence. I sipped coffee. He studied the pink skin around the scab on his knee. Finn snored.

"Someone murdered your husband."

"They did," I replied.

"Why?"

Oh dear Lord. How to answer that? "It's complicated." Henry had known people's secrets and used those secrets against them. I dared a quick glance at Beau. He'd asked a question, and I hadn't really answered.

He stared straight ahead. "Were you sad when he died?" Another tough question.

"We weren't happy together, but I was sad. I knew Grace would miss her father, and it's awful when someone is murdered."

Beau winced. "Grace says I should think about the good stuff. With my mom, I mean."

"Grace is smart that way."

"Look!" He pointed to the front walk, and my heart stopped.

My limbs froze. My blood ran cold. My heart squeezed an erratic beat when Beau bounced out of his chair. "Beau! What are you doing?"

"It's a snake."

I was aware. "If you don't bother it, maybe it'll slither away." Logic was my friend.

"But it's so cool."

Cool? There was nothing cool about snakes. The mere thought of a snake sent shudders down my spine. And now there was a scaly, hissing killer in front of us. Where was a hoe when I needed one?

Beau descended the front steps.

"Stop!" I squeaked. "Where are you going?"

"To see the snake."

What madness was this? "Please, don't."

"You're scared?" The way I'd drawn my knees up to my chin was probably his first clue. His brows lifted. How could a grown-up be afraid of a slithery black serpent with yellow stripes down its back?

Easily. "I'm terrified."

"It's a garter snake."

"It's a snake."

"It won't hurt you."

"It's a snake." This was why I didn't like the country. "Please, Beau? Leave it alone."

"Really?" He sounded disappointed.

Forget snips and snails and puppy dog tails, little boys liked snakes. "I don't want anything to happen to you."

"It's a garter snake."

"You keep saying that, but all I see is a horrifying reptile with fangs."

His forehead creased. "You're really worried about me?"

"Very."

A frog's deep ribbit rumbled through the morning, and Finn lifted his head and noticed the snake.

Woof!

The snake noticed Finn and hissed.

"Beau, back away." I leapt from my chair and raced down the steps.

Woof!

I grabbed Beau's arms and jerked him away from the snake.

"Garter snake."

"Snake."

Woof!

I levitated with Beau in my arms. One second we were in the grass, mere feet from the snake. The next we landed on the porch as I prayed that snakes couldn't climb stairs. My heart beat hard enough to bruise the inside of my chest. "Are you okay?" I demanded.

"Garter snake."

Finn danced around the hissing serpent.

"Finn."

Not surprisingly, he ignored me.

Woof! Max raced toward his friend.

"Max! No!" My pulse sprinted toward a finish line surrounded by black dots. No! I could not pass out. Could not. Would not. I had to take care of Beau. And the idiot dogs. Also, if I fainted, I'd be on the ground. With the snake. I drew air deep into my lungs and tried to calm my racing heart.

A garter snake. That's what Beau kept saying.

Not poisonous.

But what if Beau was wrong?

"Ellison?" Mrs. Smith stood in the doorway to the house. Her gaze took in the snake, the dogs, and my death grip on Beau's shoulders. "Still afraid of snakes?"

"Yep."

"It's harmless," she replied. "Max!"

My dog looked over his shoulder at her.

"Leave it."

He backed away from the snake.

"Finn!" Her voice was filled with confidence, but Finn ignored her.

Instead, he danced around the angry snake.

"Finn!"

The dog spared her a reluctant glance.

"Leave it!"

Finn whined.

"Leave it."

His stubby tail drooped, but he backed away from the snake.

The snake slithered into the grass, and I drew a clear breath.

I peeled my fingers off Beau's narrow shoulders. Hopefully, I hadn't gripped him too tightly.

He turned and looked at me. "You were afraid."

"Yes." Terrified.

"For me."

"Yes. I care what happens to you. I care about you."

He considered my words as the toe of his right sneaker tried to rub its way through the porch. A small—tiny—smile touched his lips, but he remained silent.

"Ellison."

I shifted my gaze away from Beau to Mrs. Smith.

"Your mother called last night after you'd gone to bed. She asked that you call her as soon as you got up."

What fresh hell was this? "Did she say what she wanted?"

Mrs. Smith lifted her left brow at my foolish question.

"I'll call her, but I need more coffee."

Mrs. Smith nodded as if she understood my reluctance to deal with Mother before I was fully caffeinated. "You're sure the snake wasn't enough of a wake up?"

"Very funny." The snake was enough to send me to the safety of my bed for the rest of the day.

Mrs. Smith planted her hands on her hips. "As for you, young man—"

Beau stiffened.

"I make the best pancakes in the county. Would you like some?"

Beau looked at me and grinned. An actual grin. Then, he nodded. "Yes, please."

Waiting for Mrs. Smith to put a short stack of pancakes on the table in front of an eager Beau was no hardship. I sipped coffee—guzzled coffee—and procrastinated.

Beau took his first bite and moaned his approval.

Mrs. Smith wiped her hands on her apron and offered him a gratified smile.

"I should call Mother." I made no move toward the phone.

Mrs. Smith gave an apologetic nod. "Before she calls here."

Ugh. Mrs. Smith was right. Mother had requested a call. If I didn't phone her soon, I'd annoy her. And an annoyed Mother was best avoided.

I picked up the kitchen extension and dialed.

"Walford residence."

"Good morning, Penelope. This is Ellison calling. May I please speak with Mother?"

"One moment, Mrs. Jones." At least Mother's housekeeper knew my last name.

I heard the gentle click of a receiver being placed on the counter and the sound of receding footsteps.

What could Mother possibly want? Whatever it was, I probably wouldn't like it. I watched Beau pour more maple syrup on his pancakes and pondered the unpleasant possibilities.

"Ellison." Mother's voice had me adjusting my posture. Spine straight. Shoulders back. Chin lifted.

"Good morning, Mother."

"Your sister is arriving a day early. Tomorrow, instead of Monday." Mother made it sound like a huge personal inconvenience. "I thought you'd want to know since she's staying with you."

"Thank you."

"Also, I'm planning a dinner."

"Oh?"

"Tomorrow night. To welcome Karma to Kansas City. You'll need to leave the farm early to make it on time."

"Mother, can't we do this on Monday?"

"The club is closed on Monday."

"There are restaurants."

"We're dining at the club, Ellison."

I swallowed a sigh. "Who's coming to this dinner?"

"A small gathering. The family and Libba and Charlie."

"She called you."

"Yes." Mother's tone was as flat as one of Beau's pancakes. "We must put paid to these ridiculous rumors at once." Now her insistence on the club made more sense. Everyone who counted would see Mother's support for Charlie. And if someone who counted wasn't there, they'd hear about it from those who were.

A surge of affection for my imperious, difficult, altogether terrifying mother warmed my heart. "We'll be there. What time?"

"Six. Don't be late."

"We'll see you then."

"And, Ellison."

"Yes?"

"Make sure Grace wears something appropriate."

CHAPTER SEVEN

"Grace, those are nice earrings." Better than nice. They were Akoya pearls, a gift from Mother on Grace's sixteenth birthday.

We'd arrived at the club, stepped inside the entrance, and Grace had announced she needed to go to the locker room to fetch her earrings.

"Where's the necklace?"

"In my locker."

"Those are lovely pearls."

"Which is why I took them off before swim practice." She used that *duh* tone I was so fond of.

I resisted pinching the bridge of my nose. "But you left them in your locker."

Grace stared at me as if she didn't grasp the issue. The issue was simple—if Mother discovered that Grace had left those pearls in a locker, I'd get lectures on responsibility until Grace got married. I shuddered.

"What's the big deal?"

The big deal? Sometimes it seemed like Grace and I spoke different languages.

"Go get your pearls, then meet us in the dining room." I used my I'm-at-the-end-of-my-patience voice. The ultra-calm voice that presaged a melt-down.

Grace rolled her eyes.

If a sixteen-year-old Ellison had rolled her eyes at Mother, she wouldn't have reached seventeen.

While I'd appreciate more respect (even a smidge), I didn't want Grace to fear me. I'd happily tolerate the occasional eye roll if it meant we had a more positive relationship than the one I had with Mother when I was Grace's age. With that in mind, I bit my tongue.

"Grace, cut your mom some slack."

We both looked at Anarchy in surprise. Never, not once, had Henry, my late husband, taken my side in a mother-daughter argument.

"She's trying to keep everyone happy."

He wasn't wrong.

But that didn't stop Grace from rolling her eyes so far back in her head she probably saw her brain. "By everyone, you mean Granna."

"No, I don't. We left the farm early so your mother could buy you a new dress."

"Because Granna doesn't like my taste in clothes."

"You could have worn one of the dresses she does like that's already hanging in your closet," Anarchy replied.

I didn't need Anarchy to fight my battles, but his willingness to step into the fray made my heart swell until my chest ached.

Grace crossed her arms and gave off even more attitude. "I don't see why Granna gets to decide what I wear." So. Much. Drama.

"She doesn't," I replied. "You wear what you like ninety-nine percent of the time. But tonight, when she's hosting a nice dinner, you can wear something that won't send her into a righteous tizzy." It was an entirely reasonable request.

"It's not fair."

Fair? Oh. Please. "Grace, if your biggest complaint is that you have to wear a new Lilly Pulitzer dress to dinner at the country club, you've got the world by the tail. Now, go get your pearls."

She couldn't argue my excellent point, so she extended her lower lip in a toddler's pout.

Grace wasn't this spoiled. Not even close. Her behavior reminded me of her whining on the way to the farm. Was she behaving like Veruca Salt for Beau's benefit? To distract him from the coming dinner?

I snuck a peek at Beau, who grinned as if having an obnoxious older sister was the best thing that ever happened to him.

I found a conciliatory tone. "Grace, please go get the pearls, then join us in the dining room."

"Fine." She stomped down the hallway as if the trip to the locker room was a huge imposition.

"Do I look okay?" Beau sounded nervous. Poor kid. Dinner with Mother was enough to strike fear into the hearts of grown men.

"You look marvelous," I told him. "Very handsome." He wore khaki pants, a pink gingham shirt, a navy blazer, and loafers. An outfit very similar to Anarchy's.

The three of us walked past the door to the kitchen, and I heard Mother's voice. "I don't want a paltry flame on the cherries jubilee. I want a flame I can see."

My steps slowed. "Perhaps, I should—"

"Nope." Anarchy claimed my elbow and pulled me onward. "Let your mother handle the chef."

"He may spit in our food."

Beau's face twisted in horror. "People do that?"

Anarchy barked a laugh. "We are talking about Frances Walford."

Did that mean the chef wouldn't dare, or he'd spit extra hard?

KILLING ME SOFTLY 75

With that question rattling in my brain, I let Anarchy guide me down the hallway. "I wonder why Mother picked cherries jubilee?"

"Does Karma like cherries?"

"Daddy doesn't. I don't." Marjorie, my sister in Ohio, didn't. Chances were good Karma disliked them, too. But Mother had apparently pre-ordered dessert for the table.

"Ellison."

I turned and faced Mother, who nodded at Anarchy and Beau.

"I'm glad you're here," she said. "Your father is picking up Karma at the airport, and I need to check the table."

Check the table? I frowned. Why did she need to check the table? That seemed like a lot of effort for a family dinner, even if Libba, who was as good as family, and Charlie were joining us. Mother was up to no good. "Who else is coming?"

"A couple of doctors from the hospital." Mother used her airy voice. "It's so important to show our support for Charlie."

"I wish you'd told me. I'd have left Grace and Beau at home."

"It's Karma's welcome dinner."

Not if Mother had invited a bunch of doctors. I had a sudden suspicion. "Are the doctors you invited single?"

A faint pink colored Mother's cheeks.

So, yes.

"It won't hurt Karma to meet a few eligible bachelors."

"You can't give her one day before you begin matchmaking?"

Mother's lips thinned and she lifted her chin. The better to look down her nose at me.

I'd received that exact look so often that I was immune, but Beau clutched my hand. Mother's I'll-crush-you-like-a-Styrofoam-cup expression was rather frightening. Especially if you didn't see it every day.

I gave Beau's fingers an encouraging squeeze. "Did you invite anyone else?"

The color on Mother's cheeks deepened.

"Who else?"

"Hunter Tafft."

Oh dear Lord. "You didn't." Hunter and I had a...flirtation before I fell in love with Anarchy.

"Hunter has to eat." Mother sounded defensive. Perhaps she realized she'd overstepped.

"How many are attending our family dinner?"

"Fourteen."

"Grace and Beau can eat in the snack bar."

"It won't hurt them to attend an adult dinner party."

Hurt them? No. Bore them silly? Definitely. "This is not what we discussed."

"Plans change, Ellison." She brushed past me as if we had nothing left to discuss.

I followed her into the formal dining room where plush carpet, creamy paint, and crystal chandeliers set an elegant stage for Mother's party. The table was set for fourteen, and three silver Revere bowls overflowing with white roses were evenly placed along its length. There were place cards. Place cards. And Champagne chilling in silver buckets.

Had Mother lost her mind? Charlie drinking Champagne when his patients were dropping like flies wouldn't go over well. I whispered as much.

Only a tautness near her mouth revealed I'd made a point she hadn't considered. "Tell him not to drink the wine."

"You tell him. This is your party."

"Ellison." My name on her lips was a warning.

I moved away, noting where she'd seated me—between Charlie and Dr. Abrams.

Anarchy, Libba, and the kids were seated at the far end of the table. Karma was sandwiched between Hunter and Rick Lawson.

Was it too late to back out? With Mother standing there, and with diners who were already seated at other tables openly staring at us, the answer for Anarchy and me was regrettably yes. But I could save Beau and Grace. I waved over a waiter and asked him to remove the kids' places.

"Ellison." Mother was miffed.

"The kids can eat downstairs."

She noticed the other diners gawking and capitulated. "Fine. But we'll discuss this later."

I had no doubt. With a nod, I sent Grace and Beau to the snack bar. Then I asked. "What time was Karma's plane due?"

Mother checked the elegant gold watch on her wrist and frowned. "They should be here by now."

"Does Karma know her welcome party has become a staff meeting for the single cardiologists at St. Mark's?"

"Randal Vance is bringing his wife."

"One married doctor."

"It's not my fault these men can't stay married."

If I moved halfway across the country, I wouldn't want my first night in my new home to include a dinner with men Mother deemed eligible. "Does Karma know about the additions?"

"Why must you be so difficult?"

I was definitely the difficult one. "I'll take that as a no."

Libba and Charlie's arrival precluded whatever cutting reply posed on the tip of Mother's tongue.

Ten minutes later, everyone had arrived.

My arms circled Karma for a quick hug, and I took the opportunity to whisper, "I'm sorry."

"For what?" she whispered back.

"This is not a family dinner."

"Should I be worried?"

"Probably."

Grace gave her aunt a long hug, then she and Beau, both suitably grateful, left for dinner at the snack bar.

I took my seat at the table and made polite conversation with John Abrams. John had high cheekbones, bright blue eyes and a runner's build. If I were being uncharitable, I'd call him stringy. Also, he was nearing sixty, and his hair was thinning. No. That was too charitable. His hair was gone, and he'd combed the remaining strands over the top of his head. If Mother's plan had been to create a buffet of single men for Karma, she'd miscalculated with John Abrams.

"My ex-wife is a fan of your work," he said.

And he wasn't? I never knew how to respond to backhanded compliments. "That's nice to hear."

"I understand your paintings are quite popular."

"I try." Clearly my career as an artist held zero interest for him. "How long have you been at St. Mark's?"

"Thirty years." His gaze wandered across the table. "I'm glad your mother got Charlie to come out tonight. It's never easy to lose a patient, but Charlie's taking the recent deaths especially hard."

"Oh?"

"Patients die. That's part of being a doctor. We do our best to help those in our care, but people die. We all have to go sometime."

"No one wants to go early."

"You're right." He glanced around the table. "Charlie is a good man and a good doctor."

I could hear the "but," hovering near the tip of his tongue. I said it for him, "But?"

"Those men shouldn't have died."

My stomach twisted. "And you blame Charlie?"

"No! Not at all. I don't know who to blame." He gave a little laugh. "From what I hear, you're familiar with premature death."

I gave him a tight, unhappy smile.

John's eyes twinkled. "Not your favorite topic?"

"Not remotely."

"Death is never easy to talk about, but it's a part of life."

"Not murder. Murder is outside of the natural order."

"Ellison," Mother called. "What are you and John whispering about?"

She'd have my head if I replied with the truth. "Uh…"

"We were discussing Ellison's art," said John. "My ex-wife is a fan."

"I see." Mother pursed her lips, gave me a narrow-eyed stare, then returned her attention to Hunter, who was seated to her right.

"Thank you," I told John.

"Your mother is formidable."

It was an excellent description.

His bright gaze shifted from Mother to Karma. "Tell me about your sister."

"What about her?"

"Why did she move to Kansas City? Aren't things awkward for her?" Wow. John had obviously heard the gossip about Karma being Daddy's illegitimate daughter. And he didn't pull his punches.

"Only if we let them be awkward." My tone was desert dry.

"Frances Walford won't allow awkwardness?"

"She will not." I perused the menu. "Do you know what you're having?"

Dinner went surprisingly well. I had the sole. It was excellent.

John assured me it was heart healthy.

When the waiters had cleared the last plates, Mother stood. "I took the liberty of ordering Karma's favorite dessert, cherries jubilee, for all of us." If anyone in the dining room had missed Frances Walford, her family, and the passel of well-respected doctors dining with Charlie, a flaming dessert would grab their attention.

A sous chef wheeled out a cart holding twelve sundae dishes

filled with vanilla ice cream, a large glass bowl of cherries soaked in orange juice and sugar, and a bottle of brandy. The man gave Mother a nervous smile, poured brandy over the cherries, then lit a match.

The cherries erupted in a brilliant—a blinding—flash.

Flames reached for the ceiling. And the chef's apron. Where they caught.

Somewhere in the dining room, a woman screamed.

So did the chef. And his scream was pitched higher. He slapped ineffectually at his burning clothes and hopped from foot to foot.

Everyone at the table was too shocked to move. Except for Anarchy. He launched himself out of his chair, tackled the chef, and together they rolled on the carpet.

My stunned brain restarted, and I stood, grabbed a champagne bucket, and dumped ice water on them.

Diners at other tables gawked. A woman sobbed. A young couple rushed their child away from the ongoing disaster.

I grabbed the second ice bucket and thoroughly doused the chef.

"The fire is out," he spluttered as water dripped down his face.

I knelt next to him on the ruined carpet. His apron and chef's coat were blackened. "Are you badly burnt?"

He patted his chest, then shook his head. "No."

"Thank heavens. Anarchy, are you okay?"

"I'm fine." But his navy blazer needed replacing.

I returned my attention to the slightly charred chef. "What happened?" Cherries jubilee didn't usually endanger lives.

"Your mother wanted flame. We poured Everclear over the cherries before we brought them out."

Oh dear Lord. Who'd decided grain alcohol was a good addition?

I glanced at Mother. Her cheeks were pale, and her expression was...guilty.

She caught me looking, and her eyes narrowed. If I knew what was good for me, I wouldn't speculate on her involvement.

"You're sure you're not hurt?" Anarchy asked the chef.

Charlie joined us on the floor. "Let's get you someplace where you can take off the apron and your shirt. Then we'll see how bad the burns are."

The chef looked slightly green. "Stop. Drop. Roll. I should have remembered." He stood. Slowly. Then he extended his hand to Anarchy, who'd also stood. "Thank you. You probably saved my life."

"You'd think one of the doctors would have reacted faster." Karma extended a hand and helped me off the floor.

The chef turned to me. "Good thinking with the ice water. Thank you."

"You're welcome."

"Let's get you checked out." Charlie led the chef toward the men's room.

Karma, Anarchy, and I stared at the sodden, charred carpet. Those remaining in the dining room stared at us.

I lowered my voice to barely a whisper. "I'm surprised Mother even knows what grain alcohol is."

Karma's brows rose. "It was her idea?"

"I suspect."

"Oh. Wow."

The fire had been sudden and violent and potentially deadly, and now that it was out, and no one was seriously hurt, I had a terrible urge to laugh.

I glanced again at Mother. Daddy and Hunter (how convenient to have a lawyer at the table) stood beside her as they held a whispered discussion with the red-faced club manager. None of them looked happy.

Karma giggled.

"Don't. Please, don't." If she started laughing, I would too. And Mother would never forgive me.

Libba joined us with a dessert martini clutched in her hand. "Mission accomplished. Even when Frances fails, she succeeds. This will deflect attention from Charlie."

Not in a way Mother would appreciate.

"We're lucky that Anarchy's a hero."

Anarchy blushed, and I lifted onto my toes and kissed his pink cheek.

Libba turned to Karma. "I hear you bought the Gilman's house."

"I did."

Libba lifted her glass in a one-woman toast. "When do you close?"

Karma offered me an apologetic smile. "Not for three weeks."

"Let's go to lunch tomorrow," said Libba. "We'll celebrate."

"I can't," I replied.

Libba waved away my refusal. "Of course you can. It's Karma's first day as a Kansas Citian. We'll go to Nabil's." She named one of my favorite restaurants.

"Karma?" I asked. "Are you available?"

"Sure," she said. Then her gaze landed on the destroyed carpet, and she giggled again.

"Please," I begged. "Don't laugh."

"It's just—" she covered her mouth with her hand as if the press of her fingers might smother her laughter.

"What?" Libba demanded.

Karma glanced quickly at Mother. "I have no idea where Frances got the idea cherries jubilee is my favorite. I don't even like cherries."

I too glanced at Mother. She looked angry enough to murder

the club manager or maybe have him fired. The jury was still out. "I'd better go over there."

That earned me my own one-woman toast. "You're a brave woman, Ellison Jones." If Libba wasn't careful, she'd need to return to the bar for another martini.

I approached the group at the end of the table with Anarchy at my side.

"How's the chef?" Hunter asked.

"He seems fine," Anarchy replied. "Charlie's checking him out."

Mother ignored us. Her gaze remained fixed on the club's manager. "How did this happen?"

"I assure you, Mrs. Walford, nothing like this has ever happened before."

Because no one had ever added Everclear to the cherries before. I was betting they never would again.

"My party was ruined."

The manager sighed, and I got the impression they'd already discussed Mother's ruined party. At length.

"Mother…" She was the one who'd insisted on a flame she could see. If, and that was a big if, she hadn't insisted on the Everclear, she'd bullied the kitchen staff into coming up with a way to make the flames more visible.

And boy-oh-boy had they been visible.

"What, Ellison?" Mother's annoyance bled into her tone.

"Perhaps we should retire to the veranda for an after-dinner drink. I think we could all use one."

She spared her traumatized guests a brief glance, then nodded. "Good idea."

"Mom!" Grace and Beau stood at the entrance to the dining room. Grace's shoulders relaxed when our gazes met.

I hurried toward her.

"We heard there was a fire."

"A slight mishap with the cherries jubilee."

She took in the disaster at our table and the ruined carpet. "And you said Granna's dinner would be boring."

Mother glared at me.

Karma laughed out loud.

I couldn't help myself. I joined her.

CHAPTER EIGHT

I was late. My appointment had run long, and parking on the Plaza was a bear.

Karma and Libba were already seated when I rushed into the restaurant. Smoothing the skirt of my linen shift, I slid into the open chair. "Sorry! So sorry."

Libba checked her watch and pretended affront. "You're four minutes late, Ellison. What would Frances say?"

Mother would deliver an impassioned lecture on punctuality. If I was lucky. More likely, she'd pin me with a half-despairing, half-angry gaze and tell me I was a disappointment. "Let's not go there."

"You're never late."

"Parking. Again, my apologies. Have you looked at the menu?" Chicken in lemon sauce with capers—that's what I ordered at Nabil's. Without fail. "I already know what I'm having."

Libba peered at me over the top of her menu. "It wouldn't hurt you to try something new."

Not a chance. "I know what I like."

"Do you have a favorite?" Karma asked Libba.

"I never order the same thing twice." She made fickleness sound like a virtue.

"What if you find something you like?"

Libba flitted, liked some gorgeous, slightly demented butterfly, never staying with one thing for long. Never the same entrée, never the same man for more than a few months.

Libba took a sip of wine. How long had she been waiting to already have wine? "What if there's something better waiting to be discovered?"

"Should I tell Charlie?"

My best friend, who knew no shame (she'd once taken a firefighter fifteen years her junior to a cocktail party at the club), flushed and shifted in her chair. "No need. Charlie is a keeper."

Charlie was good for her. The right age, the right profession, and the right attitude (not every man could handle Libba).

"Last night's dinner was quite something," Karma was kind. She'd obviously noticed that Libba was uncomfortable and had decided to change the subject.

"A huge success," Libba agreed.

Karma lifted her brows. By normal measures, last night's dinner was an unmitigated disaster. The chef had caught on fire, and I'd doused people with the water from the bottom of the champagne buckets.

But we weren't using normal measures. I quickly scanned Nabil's intimate dining room. The tables were covered in white linen and nestled so close that eavesdropping was a given. We were lucky. The table next to us was still empty, and the women closest to us had the look of small-town ladies who'd come to Kansas City for a special day on the Plaza. Still, I lowered my voice when I said, "The dinner served three purposes. To welcome you to town." I ticked off a finger. "To show Mother's support for Charlie." I ticked a second finger.

"Wait." Karma held up a finger to stop my count. "Why does Charlie need Frances's support?"

Libba's down-turned lips and the hunch of her shoulders spoke of her ongoing worry. "He's lost a few patients recently."

"And people are talking?"

"Worse," Libba replied. "They're whispering."

Karma's expression tightened as if she well understood the insidious nature of whispers. "Now they're talking about the fire at the club instead. What was the third purpose?"

She didn't realize? Libba and I exchanged a loaded glance. Then, I told her, "To introduce you to single men,"

"What?" Karma reared back in her chair. "That can't be right. I've barely arrived in Kansas City. Besides, I'm not interested in dating right now."

"Mother is unconcerned with your timeline, and she's decided you need a man. I suggest you draw a deep line in the sand. If you don't, she'll take over your life."

Libba smirked at me. "Because your line is so deep and well-drawn?"

"Do as I say, not as I do," I replied. Although, if Libba were being fair, she'd admit that I'd gotten much better about resisting Mother's influence.

Karma pressed her palms to her cheeks. "So those men last night—"

"Men who happen to work with Charlie," said Libba. "They're available. If you're interested, Rick Lawson is a decent prospect, but John Abrams?" She wrinkled her nose and shuddered.

"What's wrong with Dr. Abrams?" I already knew the answer. Too old. Too scrawny. Too boring. And the comb-over. Dear Lord, the comb-over.

"He wasn't thrilled when Charlie arrived. No one in the department was. They expected the new head to come from within." Libba took another sip of wine. "Instead, the hospital brought in a hot-shot doctor from Dallas."

"Charlie?" Karma confirmed.

Libba nodded. "Charlie. In fairness, Dr. Abrams seems to have gotten over his disappointment. Charlie says he's been supportive lately."

"Last night, he said the recent deaths weren't Charlie's fault."

Libba nodded her agreement. "Be that as it may, John is too old for Karma."

"He was the skinny one?" asked Karma.

"That's right," I replied. "Rick is younger and better looking."

"And Rick still has his hair," Libba added.

"They're both divorced?"

Libba swirled the wine in her glass. "Too many pretty nurses."

Now Karma wrinkled her nose. "If they're still practicing medicine, the problem hasn't gone away."

Libba lifted her glass to her lips, where her grin was beyond naughty. "That leaves Hunter Tafft."

Karma blushed a becoming shade of pink

"You like him!" Libba sounded triumphant.

Karma shot me a guilty glance.

She had no reason to feel guilty. I adored Hunter. As a friend. And I'd adore them as a couple. I'd explain that later, without my wine-guzzling friend adding color commentary.

"I noticed you and Mr. Tall-Silver-and-Handsome were deep in conversation when the chef flambéed himself. What were you talking about?"

"Hunter invited me downtown to show me around."

"Why would you want to do that?" Libba sounded genuinely curious. "The good shopping has moved south to the Plaza." Her expression turned dreamy. "Ellison, do you remember when we were girls and our mothers would take us to Emery, Bird, Thayer?"

"Of course." I loved EBT and going downtown to shop had been a special treat.

"The store closed?" asked Karma.

"They couldn't seem to keep pace with changing tastes," I explained. "Gone but not forgotten."

"As I was saying." Libba picked up her dropped thread. "There's no reason to go downtown, unless—" she waggled her eyebrows "—you want to see the view from Hunter's office in private." I kicked her under the table, and she glowered at me. "What?"

"Let's find something else to talk about."

"Fine. Did Frances tell the kitchen to put Everclear in the cherries?"

Oh, good. She was done putting Karma on the spot. It was my turn. "She's not saying."

Libba smirked. "That's as good as a yes."

"Speaking of Frances." Karma offered me a rueful smile. "What does she think of Beau?

"She's convinced I'll get my heart broken. That either Whit Riley or Beau's aunt will take him from us."

"What are you going to do?"

"We'll ask Hunter for a referral for a family law attorney."

"And then?"

"If Beau wants us, we'll adopt him."

"Of course he'll want you." Karma's voice held a wealth of certainty.

Libba put her wine glass on the table and stared at me. "You're sure?"

"Yes."

"Because Grace is almost finished with high school."

"Don't remind me."

"Your nest could be empty."

"Beau needs us. And…" I didn't have the words to explain what I felt. That Beau was *meant* to be a part of our family. That both Anarchy and I already loved him as our own. That he fit perfectly into our household. That we needed him.

"What?" Libba demanded.

"We need him." So simple. So true.

"How so?"

"That little boy is special. He brings sunshine."

"Because your life was so dark?"

I'd never wanted for food or shelter, but before I met Anarchy, the only lights in my life were Grace and my art. Now, my husband brightened every nook and cranny. "Beau brings a sweetness that was missing."

Libba reclaimed her wine glass. "Well, if you're certain." Her tone implied I was making a huge mistake.

"I've seldom been more certain."

She took another sip of her wine, took stock of those sitting around us, then said, "There's something I need to tell you."

"About Beau?"

"No."

Before she could say for more, the waiter appeared next to our table. "Are we ready to order?"

Libba looked almost grateful for his interruption.

"The chicken in lemon sauce, please." I handed him my unopened menu.

"I'll have the same," said Libba. I was one hundred percent certain she'd had the chicken before. So much for never repeating a meal.

"Make that three," said Karma.

The waiter made a note on his pad. "More wine?"

Libba glanced at her near empty glass. "Bring a bottle."

"Right away, ma'am."

Libba winced at the ma'am.

A whole bottle? I waited until the waiter walked away, then asked, "What's wrong?"

She glanced at her lap and sighed. Deeply. "You'll think I'm nuts."

"So nothing new."

"Very funny." She drained her wine glass.

Karma reached for Libba's free hand and gave it a squeeze. "What's wrong?"

"I think I saw Olivia."

"Who's Olivia?" asked Karma.

"Charlie's first wife," Libba explained. "She's been following me."

Karma and I stared at her. Libba wore a red wrap dress. A series of gold chains covered her neck and exposed chest. Her hair was perfect. Her nails were immaculate. She looked confident and sexy and powerful. Except...her eyes. There was an unfamiliar shadow in her eyes. And she held her shoulders stiffly.

"You think I'm crazy."

Yes. Completely. "Why do you think she's following you?"

"I keep seeing her. Everywhere."

I sat back in my chair. "Explain."

"I recognized her from the pictures in Charlie's photo albums of the kids. She's pretty in a Texas way."

Karma's forehead puckered. "What does that mean?"

"Big hair. Big eyelashes. Big smile," Libba replied.

"Everything's bigger in Texas," I added.

Libba scowled at her empty glass. "She is very pretty. Blonde hair—"

"Big blonde hair."

Now she scowled at me. "Big blonde hair, big blue eyes. Big..." Libba's hands hovered over her breasts.

"We get it. But what makes you think she's following you?"

"I saw her last Tuesday at the market in the produce department."

Libba at the market? I tilted my head in confusion. "What were you doing there?"

"I needed lemons and limes and olives."

The essentials for cocktails. That made sense. Libba shopping for milk and eggs did not.

"I noticed her because she looked familiar. Also, she was carrying a gorgeous Hermès bag. Truth is, I paid more attention to the bag than the woman. I didn't realize who she was until I was at Charlie's. Context, I guess. Even then, I told myself I was mistaken."

"You saw her again?"

Libba nodded. "At Swanson's on Friday. I caught her staring at me in the shoe department. Then, on Saturday, I stopped by McLain's Bakery to pick up cookies for the kids, and she was on the sidewalk."

"The same woman? You're sure?"

"Same woman. Same handbag." There were countless blue-eyed blondes in Kansas City. Very few Hermès bags.

"Have you seen her since?"

"Maybe. We had brunch yesterday at the Pam Pam Room. I thought I saw her in the Alameda lobby." She cast a grateful smile at the waiter, who appeared with a bottle of white wine—a California Chablis. Her smile widened when he refilled her glass. "Two more glasses, please."

At least she didn't plan on drinking the bottle by herself.

When the waiter left, I asked, "Why would she follow you?"

"I don't know, but I can't help but wonder if she has something to do with the kids' new we-hate-Libba attitude."

"So, she left her home in Dallas, traveled to Kansas City, and is stalking her ex-husband's new girlfriend?" Doubt laced my tone.

"Charlie says she's vindictive."

"But she doesn't know you."

"I was bonding with her children."

"Libba—"

"Don't say my name like that."

"Like what?"

"Like I've lost my marbles." She turned in her chair. "What do you think, Karma?"

"Well..."

Libba's shoulders slumped. "You, too?"

"Surely she has better things to do." Karma's tone was apologetic.

"Not really. She's an heiress. Oil wells and cattle. She doesn't have a job, and her kids are here. There's nothing to stop her from being in Kansas City."

"But that's slightly..." I searched for a word.

"Unhinged." Karma supplied.

"This is the woman who swore Charlie would rue the day he filed for divorce. She promised to destroy him."

"Why did he file?" asked Karma. "What happened?"

"It's so cliché," Libba replied. "She had an affair with the tennis pro at their country club. She's not even original. And she blamed Charlie. He spent too much time at work. He didn't pay attention to her. She was lonely. She needed companionship." Libba paled.

"What?" I demanded.

"She vowed to destroy Charlie. What if she's the one killing his patients?"

"Libba, it is possible they died of natural causes."

"You don't believe that. Anarchy doesn't believe that." She had a point. "What if it's her? What if she killed them?"

"How?" I asked. "How could Olivia kill them?" Even if Olivia's vow to destroy Charlie was real (in police work, they called that a motive), she didn't have the opportunity.

"Anarchy can figure that part out."

The waiter arrived with our glasses, and even though I hated drinking during the day, I accepted one. Some revelations simply required a sip of wine.

"You'll tell Anarchy tonight?"

"It may be late when I see him."

"What time?"

"I have book club." I turned to Karma. "I'm sorry to miss your first dinner, but I can't miss the meeting. The members are militant about attendance." Militant was a bit of an understatement. The club leaders, if they were so inclined, could successfully moonlight as dictators of small, third-world countries. "Aggie is making grilled salmon and rice and asparagus, and Anarchy and the kids will be there."

"Don't worry about it. What did you read for your book club?"

"*The Electric Kool-Aid Acid Test* by Tom Wolfe."

"Who picked that?" asked Libba.

"Celine Fowler."

"Who'd a thunk it?" said Libba. "Celine Fowler picked a book about hippies and LSD?"

"You've read it?" Surprise leaked into my tone.

"I read." Libba sounded defensive.

"*Vogue.*" I made a valid point. "*Cosmo.*"

"And books. I read that one and liked it. We're straying from the point."

"The point?"

"When will you tell Anarchy about Olivia?"

"I'll tell him," Karma offered.

Libba and I both stared at her.

She shrugged. "I'll see him at dinner. I can tell him."

"You'd do that?" Libba asked.

"Of course."

"And you won't make me sound crazy?"

I snorted, and my best friend elbowed me in the ribs.

Karma offered up a gentle smile. "You're one of the sanest people I know."

My sister needed to keep better company.

We turned our conversation toward lighter topics—fashion, Karma's ideas for redoing the kitchen in her new house, an article about women's friendships in the July issue of *Vogue*.

After lunch, we wandered across the street to Hall's.

Karma took in the pink quartz walls and elaborate iron scroll-work above the entrance and said, "So beautiful."

It was. I was so accustomed to Hall's beauty that I'd stopped seeing it. I appreciated the reminder.

Libba pushed open the glass door. "What's inside is better."

Karma bought three lipsticks in varying shades of nude.

Libba—somehow—refrained from commenting on Karma's purchases. Even as she bought a tube of fire engine red. "What about you, Ellison? You can't leave empty-handed."

"I don't need anything."

Libba gave an unattractive snort (when were snorts ever attractive?). "That's never stopped you before."

I hated when she was right. "I do need to buy a wedding gift. Do you mind?" I directed my question to Karma. I didn't much care if Libba minded. After all, I'd probably wasted months of my life waiting as she dithered over shoes or dresses or a new collar for her mink.

"Not at all," Karma replied.

"Who's getting married?" asked Libba.

"Celine and Bryce's daughter. The wedding is July twelfth."

"Pfft." After almost a full bottle of wine, Libba had no filters.

Karma tilted her head in question.

"Lots of people leave town after the Fourth," I explained. "And they don't return until Labor Day. A mid-July wedding means you can invite the world and end up with only a hundred and fifty guests."

We approached the counter, and I told the smiling woman

behind it the bride's name. "Elizabeth Fowler."

She nodded and pulled a folder from a discreet filing cabinet. "Miss Fowler is registered for Portmeirion's Botanic Garden. It's a fairly new pattern."

Which made it a bold choice. If the pattern didn't catch on, Elizabeth would have trouble finding replacement pieces. "What does she need?"

The sales associate scanned her list. "Dessert plates, cups, and saucers, and she's missing six dinner plates. How much did you want to spend?"

I gave her a figure.

"The six dinner plates?"

"Fine. You'll have them gift-wrapped and sent?"

"Of course. Your Hall's charge, Mrs. Jones?"

"Yes, please."

Libba gripped my arm hard enough to bruise. "She's here."

It took me a moment before I realized she meant Olivia. "Where?"

"Don't look."

"Then how can I see her?"

"Just trust me. She's here."

"Where?" I repeated.

"By the crystal."

Slowly, as if I were merely perusing Hall's dazzling wares, I turned my head. "There's no one there."

"She was," Libba insisted. "I swear. She was right there!" She pointed to a display of Waterford that sparkled like diamonds. "She went poof." Libba's fingers spread in a mimicry of dandelion fluff, dispersing on a strong breeze.

I didn't point out how much wine she drank with lunch. I did not note how upset she'd recently been over Charlie's troubles. I didn't question the pills she'd been taking (pills that had me worried). Instead, I lied. "I believe you."

Because, sometimes, that was what friends were for.

CHAPTER NINE

B eau needed a ride home from swim practice. So, rather than go home after lunch and an extended afternoon of shopping (after Hall's, we went to Swanson's and Woolf Brothers), I drove to the club, found a chair at a shady table near the pool, and watched the kids swim.

The coaches were hardly more than children themselves—country club swimmers who'd graduated from high school, gone to college, and come home for the summer to coach (I used the word loosely) kids at a club where their parents didn't belong. In theory, the coaches taught the youngsters how to swim. In theory. In reality, they were better at yelling encouragement than teaching proper technique.

"Come on, Beau. You got this!" A boy—young man—I didn't recognize stood at the edge of the pool and hollered for Beau to swim faster.

Hollering was not the answer.

Beau would swim faster if the coach told him to straighten his legs and bring his arms closer to his body. Maybe the coach didn't know to tell him. I resolved to help Beau with his technique. He might even get up early to swim with me. Something Grace had done exactly once.

Practice ended, and the kids emerged from the pool, sleek and brown as seals.

Beau spotted me and headed for my table. "You came." His mother had made a habit of forgetting him. Something I'd silently vowed to never do.

"I did. Do you have everything?"

"My tennis racket and sneakers are in my locker."

"I'll wait here."

Beau scurried off, leaving wet footprints on the concrete behind him.

"Ellison, I'm so glad you're here." Charlotte Simons approached me with a hopeful smile on her face. "Beck is having a slumber party this weekend, for his birthday, and we'd love for Beau to come. Nothing fancy. The boys will camp out in the backyard. Hot dogs. S'mores. Ghost stories. That sort of thing."

Charlotte was seven years my junior, and I didn't know her well. What I did know, I liked. "Thank you for including him. May I check with him before I give you an answer?"

She nodded. "Of course. That boy has been through so much. We don't want to push him. That said, we hope he'll come. It won't be the same without him."

"I appreciate that." More than I could say.

Her lips quirked. "I hear your mother hosted quite a dinner party."

"She did. It will be burned in memory forever."

Charlotte's laugh was as bright as the afternoon sunshine. "You lead an exciting life."

I wished it was boring. Truly.

Beck, who was as towheaded as Beau, joined us. "Good afternoon, Mrs. Jones." He extended his right hand.

"Good afternoon, Beck." We shook. "How was practice?"

He grimaced. "Long."

"I understand you have a birthday coming up."

"Yes, ma'am."

"Well, I hope it's a good one." What did one buy for boys? I'd need a gift whether Beau attended or not. Any boy with manners as perfect as Beck's deserved a nice present.

"Let's go, Beck." Charlotte nodded toward the path that led to the parking lot. "Ellison, I'll look forward to talking with you soon."

The boy took one step after his mother, then paused, and said, "It was nice talking to you, Mrs. Jones."

I could but hope that Grace was as polite with her elders. "Likewise. Have a happy birthday."

He grinned, then scampered after Charlotte.

"I'll phone you," I called after her. And I'd ask what Beck wanted for his birthday.

A moment later, Beau joined me with a duffel bag slung over his left shoulder. Together, we walked toward the lot.

"Did you drive the TR6?" he asked.

"I did."

"Is the top down?"

"Yes, why?"

He grinned at me. "Because it's cool." He wasn't wrong.

"Are you and Beck Simons good friends?"

"I guess. We used to have sleepovers and go to movies and stuff."

"He's having a slumber party this coming weekend."

He nodded, his face a neutral mask.

"Would you like to go?"

"I guess." Not off-the-wall excitement, but better than malaise.

"You don't have to."

Beau pushed a lock of damp hair off his forehead, and I made a mental note to get him an appointment for a haircut.

"I thought you might have fun. Everyone is camping in

Beck's backyard. Hot dogs. S'mores." Mosquitoes. Unfettered humidity.

He grunted. A grudging grunt, but I caught a gleam of interest in his eyes.

"Do you want to go?" Spending time with other boys might be good for him.

"What do I have to do?"

"Do?" I paused with my fingers on the handle of the car door. "What do you mean?"

"Do you want me to mow the grass or clean out the garage or weed the garden?"

Had pleasures been bartered in the Riley house? The more he wanted something, the higher the price?

"No. No chores." I slid behind the wheel and inserted the key in the ignition. "If you want to go to the party, you can."

I felt his side-eyed glance. "Really?"

"Really. Your only chores are keeping your room picked up and helping Anarchy take out the trash."

"You mean it?"

"I do. Should I let Beck's mother know you're coming?"

He rubbed the back of his neck and smiled. A small, secret smile. "Yes, please."

I turned on the engine. "Seat belt, Beau."

He buckled up. "Can we go back to the farm sometime soon?" Another pleasure he thought might cost him?

"You have Beck's slumber party coming up. How about the weekend after that?"

His answering grin made my heart light.

"You had fun at the farm?" He'd been quiet on the drive home. I wasn't certain if he'd enjoyed himself or not.

He nodded. "King is a good horse."

"He is."

"Grace says he likes having someone around to ride him."

"Grace is right."

"Fishing with Anarchy was fun."

They'd caught three large catfish, and Mrs. Smith had fried them for Saturday dinner.

"I'm glad he has a fishing buddy." I found fishing interminably dull.

"It's restful. It gives you time for thinking, but you still have something to do."

Something dull to do. "I'm sure Anarchy will take you again."

He nodded and fiddled with a loose thread on the hem of his polo.

He glanced my way. "How was your day?"

"Everyone asked me about the fire."

If a cadre of boys were discussing last night's dinner, it was literally the talk of the town. "What did you tell them?"

"That I missed the actual fire." He sounded disgruntled. "I just saw the chef with his clothes scorched. The most exciting thing to ever happen at the club, and I was eating fries and a milk shake in the snack bar."

Beau was wrong, Mother's fire didn't come close to being the most exciting occurrence at the club. Murder, attempted murder, and finding my first husband *in flagrante* in the coat closet during the club Christmas party all ranked higher. "I promise, the next time Mother hosts a command-performance dinner, you'll be at the table." He wouldn't thank me for it.

AT PRECISELY SIX-THIRTY, WITH A COPY OF *THE ELECTRIC KOOL-Aid Acid Test* clutched in my right hand, I rang the bell at Celine Fowler's large Tudor home.

She opened the front door with a smile. "Ellison, you're right on time, the first one here."

Mother would be so proud.

"Thank you for hosting."

"Come in, come in." She led me into the foyer. "What did you think of the book? No. Wait. Don't tell me. It's more fun when we all discuss together."

The doorbell rang, and Celine waved me toward her living room. "Please make yourself at home."

She left to answer the door, and I stepped into her living room where pale harvest-gold walls were the backdrop for modern art and French antiques. A Tabriz rug, featuring the same shade of gold as the walls, covered the hardwood floors. Celine had brought in what I assumed were her dining room chairs to create a discussion circle. At the circle's center, a coffee table held a sterling tray covered by neat rows of shortbread cookies.

I ignored the call of a comfy club chair and hung the strap of my handbag over one of the shield-back chairs (I was guessing Hepplewhite). If the discussion lasted more than a few hours, I'd pay for my choice, but the more seasoned members deserved the comfortable seats.

"Ellison." Celine stood at the entrance to the room. "Would you do me a favor?"

"Of course."

"Bryce said he'd bring out the hors d'oeuvres, but he was on a phone call. He must still be tied up. Would you please fetch them for me? They're on the kitchen counter."

"My pleasure." I walked toward the back of the house and found Celine's kitchen.

It was painted the same gold as her living room, with dark stained-oak cabinets and gold-hued tile countertops. A wall of windows with a view of the backyard and patio kept the room from feeling like a cave. An island stood at the kitchen's center, and on it rested two trays. One held a cheese ball studded with nuts and an assortment of crackers. The other held a bread bowl filled with dill dip, carrots, cherry tomatoes, and celery strips.

"Uuhh." The groan came from the floor.

For a single, precious second, I hoped that I'd imagined the noise. Then I circled the island and found Bryce.

He lay on the floor in a fetal position, clutching his left arm. Pain tightened his features into a near unrecognizable mask.

"Help me."

How? "I'll call an ambulance." I raced to the phone and dialed the operator. "This is Ellison Jones. I'm a guest at the Fowler's house. Mr. Fowler is having a heart attack." If I was wrong—I hoped I was wrong—someone could scold me later.

"The address, ma'am?"

"One-zero-one-five west fifty-seventh street. Please, send an ambulance right away."

"Help is on the way, ma'am."

"Thank you." I hung up the phone and called home.

"Jones' residence."

"Grace, it's Mom. Put Anarchy on the phone."

"What's wrong?"

"Please, Grace."

"Anarchy!" Her voice boomed through the receiver.

Five excruciatingly long seconds passed before my husband said, "Ellison?"

"Bryce Fowler is having a heart attack. I've called an ambulance. What else can I do?"

"Where are you?"

I gave him the address.

"I'm on my way. See if anyone in your book club is certified to perform CPR."

I should have thought of that. I hung up the phone and said, "Bryce, hang in there. Help is on the way."

He groaned. Low. Weak. Utterly terrifying.

"Don't die," I told him. Then I raced to the kitchen door and shrieked, "Celine!" When Celine didn't immediately appear, I stepped into the hallway. "Celine!" Louder this time. And—impossibly—shriekier.

Celine emerged from the living room looking positively scandalized. "What's wrong?" Ladies did not yell. Especially not in other ladies' houses.

"It's Bryce." I pressed my right hand over my heart. "Does anyone here know CPR?"

Celine swayed on her feet. "Where is he?"

"The kitchen."

She rushed past me. To the kitchen. Which wasn't much help unless she knew how many compressions and when to breathe.

I hurried to the living room, where I was met with curious stares. "Does anyone know CPR?"

Sarah Crawford stood. "I do. I got certified earlier this summer because I was worried about my grandchildren in my pool."

"We need you in the kitchen."

She nodded and hurried past me.

I turned to follow her, but a voice stopped me. "Ellison?"

"Yes?"

"What happened?"

"It's Bryce. I think he's having a heart attack."

Several gasps cut through the living room.

"Is he one of Charlie Ardmore's patients?"

I wasn't sure who asked, not in a room full of women, all of whom were twittering like nervous sparrows.

I ignored the question, pretended I hadn't heard it, that I didn't hear the subtext—that Charlie was to blame.

"Poor, poor Celine. What will she do without him? And, Elizabeth, the poor girl's wedding is only weeks away."

Again, I wasn't sure who'd spoken, but I was tempted to reply that Bryce wasn't yet dead. Instead, I said, "An ambulance is coming. And my husband. Would someone please let them in when they arrive?"

"Your husband? Was Bryce murdered?"

The question tightened every muscle in my back, neck, and

shoulders. Mainly because it required an answer. "I called Anarchy because he knows CPR, not because I suspect murder." Again, channeling Mother, I lifted my chin and looked down my nose. Did anyone dare ask another question? I slipped away before anyone found the courage.

In the kitchen, Celine stood next to the island and wrung her hands as Sarah knelt next to Bryce.

"His heart's still beating. It's erratic. CPR is for when a heart stops. I don't know what to do."

Neither did I.

Doctors often married nurses, and we could use a nurse right now. Too bad nurses who married up were too newly minted to be invited to join our book club. Right now, elitism wasn't working in Bryce's favor.

"Does he have any medication?" I asked. "A nitroglycerin pill?"

"Somewhere." Celine's wild gaze traveled over the tidy kitchen counters.

"Medicine cabinet?" I suggested.

"Yes!" She didn't move. Instead, she clutched the counter like a drowning woman holding a life preserver.

"Which cabinet?" If she couldn't move, I'd fetch the pills.

"Our bedroom. I'll go." Celine released her grip on the counter and stumbled toward a closed door.

"Do you need help?" I asked.

"No," she snapped, then she opened the door and climbed the backstairs.

The doorbell rang, and I hurried into the front hallway.

Wendy Holloway answered the front door.

I spotted Anarchy, and the painful tension in my neck and shoulders eased. "Back here!"

He strode toward me. "Where is he?"

"In the kitchen." I pointed.

"CPR?"

"His heart is still beating. We didn't know what to do."

Wendy opened the door a second time, and Anarchy waved at the EMTs, then led them into the kitchen.

I moved to follow, but paused when I noticed Celine careening down the front stairs.

When she reached me, she put a pill bottle in my hand. "I put down my glasses and can't see to read the dosage. Would you?"

"The EMTs are here."

"Thank, God." She pushed past me on her way into the kitchen.

I followed more slowly. The last thing I wanted to be was in the way.

"Ellison?"

I turned to Wendy.

"What can I do?" she asked.

"Thank everyone for coming, then send them home." A houseful of curious women, at least one of whom was questioning Charlie's involvement in Bryce's heart attack, wasn't ideal.

"Kick them out?" She sounded horrified.

"Politely ask them to leave."

She shook her head. "I couldn't."

I could. I moved to the entrance to the living room and felt multiple gazes land on me. I took a second to channel Mother, then said, "The EMTs are with Bryce, and I'm quite sure he'll go to the hospital. We'll need to reschedule the meeting."

No one picked up their handbag. Those who were seated remained seated. Adele Rollins reached for a cookie, then cupped her hand to catch the crumbs when she took a bite.

What would Mother do? I produced a chilly smile. "I'm sure we all want to support Celine, but guests in a crisis are a terrible distraction."

No one moved.

"It's time to go home." If that didn't work, my next option

would be unutterably rude. I was fairly sure *Get out!* would work. But my lack of decorum would also get back to Mother, and she would not be pleased. I was willing to risk it. "Ladies, it's time—"

Wendy brushed past me and collected her handbag—a raffia tote with a large peach-colored rose embroidered on the side. "Ellison's right. Celine doesn't need us. We're in the way." She hooked her bag over her elbow and headed to the front door.

Gratitude filled my heart.

With only a little muttering, the other women followed her lead, stepping aside when the EMTs wheeled a gurney into the house.

When they were gone, each and every one of them, I leaned my forehead against the front door.

"There's no reason for us to stay." Anarchy had snuck up on me.

I turned and looked up at him. Deep lines bracketed his mouth and a tightness lurked near his eyes. "Are you sure?"

He nodded "I'm sure. Sarah Crawford said she'd drive Celine to the hospital."

"While I'm grateful to avoid a trip to the emergency room, that's not what I meant. I meant Bryce. This is too many heart attacks."

Anarchy's lips thinned, and he didn't disagree.

"Did Karma tell you Libba's theory?"

"That Charlie's ex-wife is somehow responsible?"

"Ridiculous, right?"

Anarchy rubbed the back of his neck. "I'm not ruling anything out."

CHAPTER TEN

E ven in the fading light, I noticed the bag. A dispatch bag (the style made famous by Princess Grace) in Hermès's signature orange. Crafted from the finest leather and hand-stitched by generational artisans in an atelier in Paris, it was a handbag most women only dreamed of.

Every time I visited Paris, I went to the Hermès store at 24 Rue du Faubourg Saint-Honoré and tried to justify spending a small fortune for a handbag. Every time, I left the store with a scarf (or two—okay, three).

That bag…when I finally controlled my covetous drool, I noticed the woman.

Big blonde hair.

Big dark sunglasses hiding what I suspected were big blue eyes.

Big…knockers.

She wore a silk blouse, linen pants, a pirate's bounty of gold around her neck, and a diamond the size of Dallas on her left hand.

Olivia?

If so, why was she wearing an engagement ring?

The dogs tugged on their leashes. I'd slowed to inspect the bag (and the woman) and my pace had seriously lagged.

Why hadn't I waited for Anarchy to come with me? He'd been on the phone with the captain of the homicide division, and the dogs had been restless. I'd changed into walking shoes, attached leashes to collars, and headed to Loose Park. Alone. A strong, independent woman doing what needed to be done. But now, I wished Anarchy was next to me. He might not appreciate the Hermès bag (he definitely would not appreciate the Hermès bag), but he'd size up the woman.

She stared at the setting sun as if the secrets of the universe were hidden in the sky's lavenders and pinks and oranges.

Max tugged harder, and I resisted, taking the time to memorize her face—or as much of it as I could see given her dark glasses. I visualized the quick strokes of a charcoal on crisp paper. The superior set of her jaw, the slight sneer on her glossy lips, the sharp cuts of her cheekbones. The way she held her head.

Woof! Max was tired of my dawdling.

"Fine." As I walked, at the dogs' preferred pace, the drawing came together in my mind. I could do this. I could draw her, then I'd take the drawing to Charlie's, where we'd compare my drawing to his photographs. But I needed one more look.

I glanced over my shoulder. The woman was staring at me. I felt the weight of her regard. It pressed against my shoulders and pricked at my neck. Sunglasses hid her eyes, but I knew—with bone deep certainty—that her gaze held malice.

Woof! Finn lunged at a squirrel, jerking against his leash, and nearly removing my arm from its socket. I stumbled forward, barely avoiding falling face first.

Did I imagine a snicker on the evening breeze?

"Finn! Bad dog!"

He was unconcerned with my scolding.

Max simply looked amused.

I let the dogs pull me forward, eager to distance myself from the Hermès-toting woman with a death glare that rivaled Mother's.

Much to the dogs' disappointment, we skipped a second lap around the park (I had a portrait to draw) and headed home.

We slipped through the front door into the air conditioning, and I sighed. Despite the setting sun, the temperature hovered near ninety, and that didn't take the humidity into account. The house's chilled air felt heavenly.

I paused near the door to Anarchy's study, heard his voice, and unhooked the dogs' leashes.

They trotted to the kitchen, where they'd drain their water bowls then flop on the hardwoods in the spot they'd be most in the way.

"You're home." Grace greeted me from the top of the stairs.

"I am."

"We have a problem."

"Oh?"

"We need a second phone line. Anarchy has been on the phone since you left."

"Has he?"

"We'll run it to my room," she suggested. "It'll be great. You'll never have to tell me to get off the phone. The house line will be open for you."

We'd had this discussion before, and my decision was made. Not in a million years was Grace getting a private line. If we engaged a second phone line, it would be in the study. The extension in Grace's room would remain connected to the rest of the house. "I'll think about it. Where's Karma?"

"She went out for a drink with Mr. Tafft."

Mother would be pleased about that. "And Beau?"

"Watching TV in the family room."

"What's he watching?" Sumner reruns were as boring as fishing.

"Baseball."

Also as boring as fishing. "Ah. Joe Garagiola is the announcer guy." The one time I'd watched Monday night baseball with Anarchy, he'd told me the announcer was from Missouri. I remembered Missourians.

Unimpressed by my knowledge of sports or sportscasters, Grace shrugged. "I need to call Debbie."

"Give me a minute to change, then I'll find out how long he'll be."

"Thanks, Mom." No eye roll. I'd take my miracles wherever I found them.

I hurried upstairs to our bedroom and unzipped my dress. I should have changed before I walked the dogs, but they'd been so antsy. And after what happened at the Fowlers' house, I'd needed the air. I sniffed at my dress, decided it needed to go to the cleaners, and checked the pockets.

I found a pill bottle and stared at it in confusion. Then I read the label.

It was the bottle Celine had given me.

Bryce's pills.

How had I come home with them?

I must have put them in my pocket when I faced off against the lingering book club.

Well, Bryce wouldn't need the pills tonight. The hospital would manage his medications. I hoped. The alternative was too awful to consider.

I donned shorts and a scooped-neck tee-shirt, put the pills on my dresser, and ran upstairs to my third-floor studio, where I grabbed a sketchbook and a few charcoal pencils.

"Mom!" Grace stood at the bottom of the attic stairs and glared at my art supplies. "This is so lame. You said you'd ask Anarchy to get off the phone as soon as you changed."

That wasn't quite right. I'd said I'd ask him how much longer he'd be.

"I have to talk to Debbie. It's important."

I raised my brows.

"Seriously, Mom. She met this guy, and she likes him, but he goes to South." She meant Shawnee Mission South, a public high school on the Kansas side.

"So?"

"Her mom is freaking out." Grace curled her fingers and made air quotes. "She doesn't know his people." Her eyes rolled dramatically. "We're sixteen. It's not like Debbie wants to marry him, just go to the movies. Her mom needs to take a chill pill."

"Grace!"

"What? Her mom is overreacting."

Debbie's mom wasn't the only one who was overreacting.

"Debbie's upset and she needs her friends, and I can't even call her because Anarchy is hogging the line."

I didn't have it in me to argue. "I'm headed to the study now." I descended the stairs, tapped on the study door, then cracked it open.

Anarchy, who sat behind the desk, looked up from making notes on a sheet of paper. When he saw me, his eyes lit with interest. "Peters, I'll call you back." Peters was his curmudgeonly partner. He returned the receiver in the cradle. "I like those sh—"

Brnng, brn—

He stared at the phone as if he didn't believe how fast it had rung or how fast Grace had answered it.

I stepped into the room. "Grace has been waiting for a call."

He stood and circled the desk. "Sorry."

"I'll contact the phone company tomorrow. We'll have a line added in here." I'd procrastinated long enough.

"Good idea." His hands settled on my hips. "I like these shorts."

My mouth went dry.

He smiled. A satisfied smile—as if he sensed the butterflies running riot in my stomach.

"Have you heard anything about Bryce?" My voice was barely a croak.

"Critical but stable condition."

He was still alive. There was still hope. "Does Charlie know?"

"I can't answer that." He glanced at the phone. "Any chance I'm getting the line back?"

A snowball had a better chance in hell. "Let's give her a few minutes. Beau's watching baseball. We can keep him company."

"You want to watch baseball?" He sounded highly skeptical.

I wanted to put the woman's face on paper while it was fresh in my mind and being alone with Anarchy when he looked at me hungrily, as if I were his favorite dessert, was too distracting. I held up my sketchpad. "You can watch for both of us. I'll draw."

"Are you sure that's what you want?"

Lord, he was tempting. "Baseball."

Anarchy claimed my free hand, and, together, we walked to the family room, where Beau sat on the sofa engrossed in the game.

"Who's winning?" asked Anarchy.

Beau kept his gaze fixed on the screen. "The Yankees."

Anarchy's upper lip curled. Apparently, he wasn't a fan.

I turned on the lamp next to my favorite club chair, settled in, took a much-needed calming breath, and drew. First, the shape of the woman's face. Oval with a slightly painted chin. Next, her lips, her nose, her brows.

Beau peered over my shoulder. "She doesn't have eyes. It's creepy."

I'd distracted him from the game? I glanced at the television where a man with a face covered in shaving cream extolled the smoothness of his razor.

"You're right." I added a pair of Oliver Goldsmith oversized tortoise-shell sunglasses. I lost sunglasses too often to wear such an expensive brand, but I recognized them when I saw them.

"Who is she?"

"I saw her in the park."

"And you decided to draw her?"

"Yep." I replicated the glasses' tortoise-shell effect with shading.

Anarchy perched on my chair's arm and studied my drawing. "You don't usually draw people."

"My subjects are never happy. I make them look too old or too fat, or their noses or ears are too big.

"Why now?"

I glanced at Beau. "Libba described a woman to me at lunch yesterday." Anarchy would know I meant Olivia. "This might be her."

He stiffened. "She was at the park?"

"Watching the sun go down." And giving me death glares.

Anarchy's eyes narrowed and he rubbed his chin. "I wonder if Charlie's home."

"If he isn't, I can call Libba. She'd come over in a heartbeat if I told her about this." I nodded at my sketch.

"That's assuming we ever regain control of the phone line."

I swallowed a laugh.

The commercials ended, and Beau returned his attention to the game.

"Did she threaten you?" Anarchy whispered.

"Not remotely."

He raked his fingers through his hair. The man was worried.

"You don't seriously think she's killing Charlie's patients?"

"I don't know what I think."

"How would she get access? How would she know who they are?"

"Libba said she's filthy rich. She has plenty of money to bribe someone for medical records."

"Even if that's true, she can't make someone have a heart attack."

"She's an attractive woman." Anarchy stared at my drawing. "Getting close to men wouldn't be a problem. She might slip something in their drinks." Anarchy was making Libba's crazy theory seem almost plausible.

"She'd have to be a psychopath to kill men she doesn't know just to hurt her ex-husband's practice."

"Destroy his reputation, destroy him."

"What are you guys whispering about?" asked Beau.

"One of Anarchy's cases."

He winced.

The poor boy had experienced enough darkness without us discussing murder in front of him. "Who are the Yankees playing?" I didn't care, but I asked.

"The Brewers."

"They're from Milwaukee?"

The men in my family did not say 'duh,' but I could tell at least one of them wanted to.

I returned my attention to my drawing, adding a bit more shading to the cheeks, until the woman from the park was captured in my sketchpad. Satisfied, I put the drawing on the table next to my chair, stood, and opened the door to the backyard.

"Where are you going?" asked Beau.

"Just getting some air." And checking to see if it looked like anyone was home at Charlie's. I stepped onto the patio, and warm air pressed against me as fireflies twinkled and locusts droned. A perfect summer night. Made more perfect by the lights blazing from Charlie's upstairs windows.

"Pansy!" The annoyance in Charlie's voice was evident. Not surprising given that Pansy was a naughty, naughty dog. She destroyed flower beds in seconds flat. Boxwoods and large perennials took her a bit longer. Minutes instead of seconds.

I stepped into the family room and picked up my sketchpad. "Charlie's home."

Anarchy rose from the couch. "Beau, Ellison and I are going next door. We'll be back in a few minutes."

"But the bases are loaded."

"Tell me what happens when I get back. I'm hoping for a double-play."

Beau grinned. Then his gaze fixed on the TV screen, and we were forgotten.

Anarchy and I cut across our backyard, using the gate that connected our property to Charlie's. Pansy bounded toward us. *Woof! Woof!*

I pet her silken head. "Hi, pretty girl." Pansy might be naughty, but she was also gorgeous and sweet. "Charlie?"

"Here." He sat on the patio with a bottle on the table next to him and a glass in his hand. "Did Pansy destroy your hostas?"

"No."

"Your annuals?"

"No."

"What did she do?" He sounded a bit slurry. And tired.

"Pansy hasn't caused a single problem."

"Then why are you here?" Definitely slurry.

"I want you to look at a drawing."

He frowned and splashed more scotch into his glass. "Do either of you want a drink?"

I glanced at Anarchy. How many had Charlie had? "No, thank you."

I approached the table and handed Charlie my sketchpad.

Charlie stared at the page. He tilted his head. He squinted. Then he stood, taking my drawing closer to the house where the lanterns flanking the backdoor offered better light. "I don't understand."

"Don't understand what?"

"Why did you draw my ex-wife?"

I'd been expecting to hear she was Olivia, but Charlie's confirmation still left me slightly breathless. "I saw her at the park today."

"That's not possible." He winced. "Dammit. I told Libba she was wrong. That she was imagining things. We had a fight. She left in a huff."

"She told me Olivia has been following her."

"What? She never said. We've got to call her." He yanked open the back door.

"To apologize?"

"No! To make sure Olivia hasn't gotten to her."

"Gotten to her?" I asked.

"Harmed her," Charlie bit out.

What? My heart skipped a beat. "She'd do that?"

Charlie's answering laugh was dry and cynical and stole my breath. "Yes." He picked up the receiver and dialed. "It's ringing."

Anarchy folded his arms over his chest and leaned against the kitchen counter. "Olivia is violent?"

"If she thought the violence would hurt me? Absolutely." Charlie tossed my sketchbook on the counter and used his free hand to tap a staccato beat against his leg. "Why isn't Libba answering?"

"She might be out." I suggested.

"With whom?" he snapped. "It's Monday night. We should go over there. Right now. I'll grab my keys."

"How much have you had to drink?" asked Anarchy.

Charlie scowled. "I'm fine." He'd be more convincing if he didn't sway.

"That's not an answer," Anarchy replied. "I'll drive. We'll pick you up in five minutes."

"Wait."

Both men stared at me.

"What about your kids?"

"The housekeeper is here," Charlie replied. "I'll tell her I'm leaving."

I grabbed my drawing, and Anarchy and I hurried home.

When we stepped into the kitchen, I called, "Grace!"

"I'm on the phone." Her voice floated down the stairs.

"I need to speak with you."

"In a minute."

We didn't have a minute. If we didn't get over to Charlie's, he might try to drive himself. Also, Libba might be in trouble. I picked up the receiver and said, "Grace, I need to speak with you. Immediately. You can call Debbie back."

"Mom!" She was outraged.

"Now, Grace."

"Fine." She slammed the receiver into its cradle.

Seconds later, she barreled down the backstairs. "I can't believe you did that."

"Something may have happened to Libba."

"What?" The surliness melted off her face.

"Anarchy and I are leaving to check on her. Would you please keep an eye on Beau?"

"Of course. You'll let me know if she's okay?"

My stomach twisted. Libba and I might snipe and bicker, but she was the woman who was always in my corner. I prayed she was okay, that Charlie was overreacting. "I will."

"Ellison, let's go."

I followed Anarchy to his car and climbed into the passenger's seat.

"Nothing happened in the park?"

"Nothing. She scowled at me. She may have snickered when Finn yanked his leash. That's it."

We pulled into Charlie's circle drive, and he hopped into the backseat. "Drive!"

"What makes you so sure she'd hurt Libba?" asked Anarchy.

"A few things the kids have said."

"Like what?"

"My daughter seems sure that if Libba wasn't in my life, her mother and I would get back together."

"You think Olivia told her that?"

"I do."

"Is it true?"

"No! God, no. Neither of was…perfect during our marriage."

"You both cheated."

"Don't hold back, Ellison."

I wouldn't.

"With both of us untrue and unhappy, there didn't seem to be any reason to keep trying. But Olivia didn't agree. She wanted to continue on. When I insisted on a divorce, she hired an army of lawyers. She tried for full custody. She demanded a ridiculous amount in alimony. She fought every step of the way."

"Sounds expensive," Anarchy observed.

"Nearly bankrupting me with attorneys' fees was a bonus for her."

Olivia sounded like a terrible woman, even worse than Prudence Davies. And Prudence had her picture in the dictionary next to the word harpy. "Charlie, do you think Olivia would target your patients? To get back at you?"

"Oh, hell."

I waited for him to say more. When he didn't, I glanced into the backseat. Charlie slumped forward as if an enormous weight had settled on his shoulders. He'd buried his head in his hands.

I had my answer.

CHAPTER ELEVEN

"How?" I demanded. Not the nicest way to ask, but my worry for Libba precluded politeness.

Charlie, who hunched in the backseat, lifted his chin. Slowly. As if his head weighed a hundred pounds. "What do you mean?"

"How could your ex-wife kill Lee and Owen? How could she cause Bryce's heart attack? Does she have a medical degree?" Some evil superpower?

"No."

"Does she have access to drugs or a poison that might have killed them?"

"I wouldn't put it past her."

I turned my whole body to stare at him. "Seriously?"

"Seriously."

I glanced at Anarchy. His hands were tight around the steering wheel, and his lips had thinned.

"Those men were a means to an end, destroying me. In her mind, their murders are justified."

Most killers were able to justify their actions. I believed that Olivia was a terrible woman, but I still couldn't wrap my mind around how she'd caused heart attacks. "We don't even know if their deaths are murders."

"They shouldn't have died, Ellison. Not Owen. Not Lee. They had mild, manageable heart conditions." Charlie had been their doctor. He knew their medical histories.

In my far-too-extensive experience, people committed murder because their victims posed a threat—to the killer's wealth or reputation or sense of self. It was venal and unforgivable, but also understandable. This? Killing strangers to punish Charlie? This was somehow a million times worse.

Charlie leaned forward. "Can you drive any faster?

Anarchy sped up. Well past the posted limit. He was worried about Libba, too.

That made three of us.

"She's okay," I said. She had to be. The alternative might destroy me.

As if he could sense my fear, Anarchy reached for mind, giving my fingers a comforting squeeze.

I stared at the window at the houses flying past us. "If all this is true, your ex-wife is certifiable."

"Yes," Charlie agreed.

"Why did you marry her?"

"I met a gorgeous, smart, rich woman. She was charming. She was witty. She was fun at parties."

"Then what happened?"

"Life. We weren't as well-suited as I thought. The more she demanded that I be at home, the more time I spent with my patients. She became increasingly possessive. Unreasonable."

"You truly believe she'd hurt Libba?"

"I do."

I glanced at the speedometer. We weren't far from Libba's. I wouldn't give in to panic. Not yet.

"What about your children?"

"What about them? She'd never hurt the kids."

If she'd killed Owen and Lee, she'd be tried for murder. She'd be jailed as a mass murderer. That would definitely hurt her children. How did a child get over that?

My thoughts turned to Beau. At least his mother wasn't that bad.

Anarchy pulled up in front of Libba's building, and Charlie leapt from the car. He was running for the entrance before Anarchy shifted to park.

With Charlie gone, Anarchy backed the car into a parking space across from the front doors. "Will you stay here? Please?" His eyes implored me.

He wanted me to wait in the car? "What if Libba needs me?"

"I'll come get you. Please, Ellison?" If something had happened to Libba, he didn't want me to see.

"But—"

"Please."

We were wasting time.

"Fine," I ceded with a brief nod. "You'll hurry?"

He nodded and followed Charlie into Libba's building.

I rolled down the car's windows and turned off the engine. There was a fountain to the right of the building's doors, and the splash of its water mixed with the sounds of traffic from nearby Wornall Road. I closed my eyes and pressed the back of my head into the headrest. Worry for Libba churned in my stomach, and I swiped an errant tear from my cheek. I would not cry. Libba was fine.

I glanced at my watch. How long had Anarchy and Charlie been gone? It seemed like forever.

Worry gnawed at me, and I forced myself to think of something other than Libba lying lifeless on the floor of her apartment.

Had Olivia really killed Owen and Lee? Drugged Bryce? I still couldn't see how she'd pulled it off.

Anarchy and I had seen Lee the night before he died. He'd

been out for a walk, not seducing a blonde Texan. When had Olivia slipped him the poison?

Were we so eager for Charlie to be blameless that we saw murder instead of malpractice? The thought felt disloyal.

I opened my eyes and checked my watch again. A minute had passed. What was taking them so long?

Why was Olivia lurking in Kansas City and following my friend?

Maybe she had killed Charlie's patients.

My brain was a lava lamp of questions and possibilities. Unformed. Morphing. Twisting. There was also worry and fear and anxiety floating around in there. It made for a toxic soup.

A white Mercedes pulled into the small parking area in front of Libba's apartment building, and I watched as it rolled to a stop at the building's entrance.

The car's back door opened, and a woman stepped out into the light cast by enormous sconces on either side of the front doors.

"Libba!" My voice carried.

She turned.

I launched myself out of Anarchy's car, raced across the parking lot, and pulled her into a hug.

"Ellison, what's wrong? Why are you here?" She stepped back and frowned at me. "What are you wearing?"

Trust Libba to critique my clothes at a moment like this. She was almost as bad as Mother. And she was gloriously alive. "You're okay!"

"Of course I'm okay. Why wouldn't I be?"

I heard car doors opening and glanced behind me. Hunter and Karma stood on the pavement, looking every bit as befuddled as Libba.

"I'm sorry," I told her. "We should have believed you."

Libba lifted a sardonic blow. "About?"

"About Olivia. I saw her in the park. Charlie's out of his mind with worry for you."

"Charlie's worried?"

"He's afraid Olivia harmed you."

"Truly?"

"Yes. Apparently, she's dangerous."

"He's worried?" Were those stars in her eyes?

"He's upstairs right now. Looking for you." Now that I knew she was safe, annoyance crept in. "Where have you been?"

"Hunter took us to Milton's," said Karma.

Milton's Tap Room was a Kansas City institution. Its owner, Milton Morris, was a character. With his too-large glasses, receding hairline, ever-present glass of Cutty Sark, and foot-long cigar, the man had a joke or a wisecrack for everyone who entered his bar. Local legend had it that he got his start selling medicinal whiskey during prohibition. He opened his first bar the year after the eighteenth amendment was repealed. Given his history, it was no surprise that he and his wife, Shirley, didn't bother with liquor laws they deemed silly—like a minimum drinking age. Teenagers snuck into Milton's to drink beer or cheap whiskey. The kids with good taste went back for the music.

"I wanted to listen to jazz," Karma continued.

And Hunter had taken her.

"How did you end up at Milton's?" I asked Libba. It was the darkest bar in town. Not chic. Not the sort of place where the other patrons would appreciate the Pucci minidress she wore.

"I called and asked if Libba and Charlie wanted to join us," Karma replied.

"Libba!" Charlie burst out of the building and swept her into an encompassing hug. "Thank, God."

"You worried?"

"Yes, woman. Of course I worried. I love you."

Libba froze. A mosquito trapped in amber. A deer caught in

headlights. Was that the first time he'd told her? Was she breathing?

"I... I love you, too."

He kissed her. One of those 1940s movies kisses. They deserved a glorious, technicolor sunset or a night sky filled with breathtaking fireworks or waves crashing on a tropical beach. That and a lush, romantic musical score.

They got the light from the building and locusts' drones.

After a few seconds, the rest of us averted our gazes.

Mine went to the driveway, where a sedan idled near the entrance.

I narrowed my eyes. Something odd. Something niggled at me. No headlights.

Before I had a chance to say anything, the car sped toward us. So fast. Zero to sixty, with no sign of stopping.

I shoved Libba and Charlie out of the way before I jumped backward, landing on the concrete with a spine-jarring impact that stole my breath.

The car slammed into the side of Hunter's Mercedes with a sickening crunch of metal.

Time stood still.

Then Anarchy yelled, "Ellison!"

I'd answer him as soon as I my lungs inflated.

The driver shifted into reverse and, with a squeal of their tires, sped away.

"Ellison." Anarchy crouched next to me. "Are you hurt?"

Unable to speak, I shook my head.

He patted up and down my arms as if he doubted me.

I was fine. Truly. "Libba?" I croaked.

"We're okay."

Thank heavens. If I hadn't been looking the right way, at the right time, Charlie and Libba would be splatted against Hunter's Mercedes like bugs on a windshield.

I should feel anger. Someone had tried to kill my best friend. But all I felt was shaky. We'd gotten lucky. So lucky.

Anarchy took my hands and gently pulled me to standing. "You're sure you're okay?"

I nodded.

He looked over his shoulder at Hunter's crumpled car. "Did anyone see the driver's face?"

No one said a word.

"It had to be Olivia. Who else could it be? Arrest her for attempted murder." Charlie sounded cold, as if nearly losing Libba had engendered an anger so fierce it burned below freezing.

Hunter shook his head. "Anarchy needs proof before he can make an arrest."

Charlie wheeled on him. "Then he can haul her in for questioning!"

"He has to find her first."

A TOW-TRUCK ARRIVED, AND WE WATCHED AS THE DRIVER winched Hunter's mangled car.

"Please take it to Frank and Bob's in Westport," Hunter told him.

When the truck's taillights faded into the night, Charlie turned to Libba. "Go pack a bag."

She frowned. "What? Why?"

"You need a bag."

"To go where?"

"My house." He glanced at me. "Or Ellison's. You're not staying here."

Oh, dear. Libba didn't respond well to orders. Surely he knew that by now. One would think a doctor would be smarter.

She planted her hands on her hips, and a stubborn expression settled on her face. "You don't tell me what to do."

"Olivia just tried to kill you, to run you down." Charlie had no doubts as to the driver's identity. "You're not staying here alone."

"Technically, she tried to squish me between two cars, not run me down."

"Libba, I'm trying to keep you safe."

"Maybe it's not me she's after. Maybe she was trying to kill you."

"Possibly," he ceded. "But I'm not risking your safety. Pack. A. Bag."

When she didn't move, Charlie turned to Anarchy. "Tell her she's not safe here."

"Tell him he's being ridiculous."

Anarchy winced as if their argument pained him, as if he hated being put in the middle. I didn't blame him. "You're welcome at our house, Libba."

She scowled at my husband's offer of hospitality.

"Libba." I held out my hands, pleading. "I won't sleep a wink for worrying about you. Please, come home with us."

She bit her lower lip, considering my offer. "Lord knows, you need your beauty rest."

I let that slide. "When we get home, we'll split a bottle of wine and the three of us—" I nodded toward Karma "—can complain about men who demand rather than ask nicely."

Charlie flinched. Served him right.

"And then?" Libba asked. "How long am I supposed to stay at your house?"

"Until we know you're safe," Charlie replied.

"Since the threat is from your nutso ex-wife, you should be quiet."

Charlie flushed. "Libba. Please."

"Fine. I'll pack." She made staying safe sound like a huge imposition.

"Do you want some help?" I asked.

"Why not?" She sounded tough, but I saw a hint of fear swimming in her eyes.

We entered the elevator and pushed the button for her floor.

"Can you believe the gall of that man? Pack. A. Bag. Who does he think he is?"

"The man who loves you."

She leaned against the elevator's back wall. Sagged. "I could have lost him."

"But you didn't."

Her hands shook. "It was so close."

"You're both fine."

"I love him." She made it sound like a revelation.

"That's a good thing."

"Is it? What if she'd hurt him? Killed him? How could I go on without him?"

"That's the risk we all take."

"That a lover's crazy ex-wife will murder him?"

"That we might lose the people we love. But what would our lives be like without them? Dull. Colorless. Lonely."

"When did you get so wise?"

"When I fell in love with Anarchy."

The elevator doors slid open, and I followed Libba into the hallway.

She inserted her key in the door. "What are we going to do?"

"About?"

"Olivia."

"Let Anarchy find her." He would. In his mind, she'd threatened me. And he took my safety seriously.

"That's not enough." She stepped into her apartment and flipped on a light. "We'll talk to Elaine tomorrow."

Sensing a terrible plan, I was immediately on edge. "Why?"

"To ask if she ever saw Olivia near Owen. We'll discuss the same thing with Joanne."

Because they'd so appreciate Libba hinting their late husbands had been stepping out with a pretty blonde. Suggesting infidelity to grieving widows wasn't a just a terrible plan, it was an epically terrible plan.

"Shouldn't we just talk to Bryce?" A completely reasonable suggestion.

She tilted her head. "Bryce?"

"Bryce Fowler. He had a heart attack tonight. He's in the hospital."

"No!" She pressed her hands to her cheeks. "Poor Charlie."

"Poor Bryce. Poor Celine."

Olivia had a lot to answer for.

"Them, too."

I followed her into her bedroom and watched as she pulled a small overnight bag out of her closet. "That's optimistic."

"If I have to stay longer, I'll come back for more clothes."

"Can I help?"

"No." She took a fresh nightgown from her dresser drawer but made no move to put it in her bag.

"Libba?"

"She almost killed us both." Her hands shook.

"She didn't."

"It was too close."

I took the gown from her and put it on the bed. "Sit."

She collapsed onto a petite bergère covered in embroidered peach silk that matched the coverlet on her bed.

I knelt beside her and took her hands in mine. "You're okay. Charlie's okay. You'll get past this."

"Will I? I'm not like you, able to face off against a killer, then go out for dinner."

I had never, ever done that. "You need to rest. You'll feel better in the morning. I guarantee it."

"What about our hen party?"

"We'll have it another night. Besides, I think Charlie got the message. You prefer requests to orders."

"What an idiot." Her tone was fond.

"Your idiot."

"He is that." She stood and smoothed her dress over her hips. "We have a plan. Tonight, I rest. Tomorrow, we visit Bryce."

I could hardly wait.

CHAPTER TWELVE

I f someone blindfolded me, spun me three times in a circle, and set me loose in the hallways of St. Mark's Hospital, I'd find wherever I needed to go. I'd spent that much time there. Far, far too much time.

Which is why, when Libba insisted that the cardiology ward was on the second floor, I crossed my arms and said, "No, it's not."

"It is. I visited Myra Winfield there two months ago. I remember."

"Myra Winfield had appendicitis."

She frowned. "She did? Are you sure?"

"Positive."

"Fine. If you're so smart, lead the way."

I led us to the nurses' station in the cardiology unit, where a no-nonsense woman (no make-up, tight bun) regarded us from behind a counter.

I rested a bouquet of English stock and stargazer lilies on the counter and said, "We're here to see Bryce Fowler. What's his room number?"

"Pretty flowers," said the nurse.

"Thank you. I love flowers with a strong scent." The bouquet smelled heavenly.

"Especially here," said Libba.

The nurse shifted her gaze. "What's that supposed to mean?"

"Hospitals don't smell very good. Flowers help cover unpleasant scents."

The nurse's lips thinned.

"This one smells like antiseptic and clean linen." I spoke so fast my words tripped over each other.

It was too little, too late. The damage was done. A mulish expression settled on the nurse's face. She'd decided to be an impediment. "Mr. Fowler isn't allowed visitors."

"I apologize," said Libba. "I didn't mean this hospital."

"No visitors."

Libba would not be dissuaded. She poked me in the ribs. "Ellison, tell her who your mother is." As chairman of the board, Mother had a tendency to make her presence felt.

I wanted to poke Libba back. But, harder. Using my family name to get special treatment was wrong. "If Bryce is so ill he can't have visitors, we should let him rest." I offered the nurse a conciliatory smile. "You'll make sure he gets these?" I scooted the vase toward her.

She offered me a brief, you-should-be-grateful-I-agreed-to-do-this nod. "Of course. Who should I say they're from?"

"Ellison Jones."

The nurse paled. "You're Frances Walford's daughter."

"I am."

Libba grinned as if we were providing her with top-shelf entertainment.

The nurse adjusted the collar of her white uniform. "Would you like to give them to him yourself?"

Libba smirked. "You just said he can't have visitors." That attitude would not get us in to see Bryce.

KILLING ME SOFTLY 133

"There are exceptions to every rule." The dark scowl the nurse gave Libba made it clear Libba was not an exception.

"Thank you—" I checked the nurse's nametag "—Patricia."

"I'm dating Charlie Ardmore," Libba told her.

"Bully for you."

I swallowed a laugh.

"You're letting Ellison in."

"I'm sure Mrs. Jones won't overstay her welcome."

Libba drew her shoulders back. "And I will?"

"I don't know you." The glint in Patricia's eyes said she was enjoying this.

"I'm Charlie's girlfriend."

"So you say."

"Ask Ellison. She'll tell you.

"I don't care who you're dating. You're not visiting Mr. Fowler.

Libba, who realized she was fighting a losing battle, threw up her hands. "Fine. Ellison, you chat with Bryce. I'll wait for you in the coffee shop." Then she lifted her nose in the air and swanned her way to the elevator.

When the doors closed behind, Patricia asked, "Is that woman really dating Dr. Ardmore?"

"She is."

Her face scrunched as if I'd just offered her a large bowl of stewed prunes. Then she sighed and shook her head as if there was no accounting for taste. "Mr. Fowler is in room three-two-three."

I picked up the vase. "Thank you for allowing me to see Bryce." I should count this as a win. Except I was now the one who had to ask Bryce if he was involved with Charlie's ex-wife. Talk about a hollow victory.

"Ellison?"

I turned and found Rick Lawson right behind me. Too close. I took a step away from him and said, "How nice to see you."

"Likewise." He eyed the flowers. "Visiting a patient?"

"Bryce Fowler."

"One of Charlie's." He sounded almost amused.

"Yes."

"Fowler is lucky. Most of Charlie's patients end up in the morgue."

Weren't doctors supposed to actually care if patients died?

My thoughts must have shown on my face, because Rick held up his hands. "Sorry. Gallows humor."

I was married to a homicide detective. I understood gallows humor. I also understood callous disregard.

Rick adjusted the stethoscope that hung around his neck. "He seems to be doing much better. I wonder if it wasn't a touch of angina."

I'd seen Bryce in agony on the floor. Whatever brought him there had been awful. "I'm just glad he's feeling better."

"I'm sure Charlie agrees." Now, Rick sounded snide. "Interesting dinner the other night."

"It was." If he noticed the chill in my voice, he ignored it.

"Your sister is living with you?"

"For the next three weeks."

"And then?" Surely he'd heard the discussion about updating Karma's new kitchen when we had dinner.

"She bought a house."

"Did she? A little Cape Cod in Fairway?"

"No."

"A Prairie Village ranch?"

"Karma bought the Gilmans' house."

For an instant, he looked shocked. Then his expression smoothed. "Your father helped her?"

I'd never really interacted with Rick before. We chatted at the occasional cocktail party, exchanged pleasantries at the dry cleaners, nodded politely at church. I hadn't realized he was a patronizing misogynist. "Karma bought the house on her own."

"A bank gave her a mortgage?"

"She paid cash. Now—" I stepped around him "—if you'll excuse me?"

"On her own?" His disbelief was insulting.

"She's very good at her job." I glanced at the nearest room number. Three-one-seven. "She invests other people's money. Makes them rich."

"Does she?"

I didn't like the sneer in his voice. "Herself, too."

"Is she taking new clients?"

We both knew he would never invest money with a woman.

"You'd have to ask her." I walked away from him.

"Ellison?"

I paused.

"Tell Karma I'll call her."

Using one of Grace's eye rolls was so, so tempting. I resisted. "I'll tell her." Not. Likely.

I reached Bryce's door, tapped lightly, then slipped into his room.

The hale and hearty man looked too thin in his hospital gown.

"Bryce?"

He turned his head toward me and offered a weak smile.

"How are you feeling?"

"Never better."

I smiled at him. "Liar."

"It was worth a try." He rubbed a hand over his cheek and winced as if he'd just realized he needed a shave. "Thank you."

"For?"

"For everything you did. Calling the ambulance. Finding Sarah."

"It was nothing."

"It saved my life."

"Then I'm happy I was there." I put the flowers on the ledge by the window and gathered my courage. "I have something I need to ask you."

"Yes?"

I reached into my handbag, pulled out the drawing of Olivia, and showed it to Bryce. "Do you know this woman?"

He stared at Olivia's likeness for long seconds. "Never seen her before."

I believed him, but I still asked, "You're sure?"

He took another few seconds to study the picture, then gave a tiny shrug. "She's pretty. I'd remember her. Who is she?"

His question was an obvious one. I should have come prepared with an answer. "No one important."

"Then why ask me?"

I didn't have an answer for that either. "Um…"

The door opened, and Celine, who clutched a cup of coffee as if it were a lifeline, stepped into the room and saw me. "Ellison. What a nice surprise."

Wow, was I grateful for her interruption. I slipped the drawing into my handbag, then gave her a brief hug.

"How kind of you to visit." She sank onto the ugly chair next to Charlie's bed. The poor woman looked exhausted.

"I brought flowers." I nodded at the bouquet. "Is there anything I can do for you?"

"Me? No. I'm fine." She wasn't fine. She looked almost brittle.

"You're sure?"

"I'm sure. We need to take care of Bryce."

The door swung open—for a man who wasn't supposed to have visitors, Bryce's room was as busy as Grand Central—and Charlie stepped inside. He frowned at me for a full ten seconds before turning his attention to his patient. "How are you this morning?"

"Achy and tired."

Charlie nodded as if he expected Bryce's answer.

"When can I go home?"

Charlie glanced at the chart in his hands. "Your blood work looks good, but you're not fully recovered. Plan on staying with us for a few more days."

"I'd be more comfortable at home."

I shouldn't be privy to this conversation.

"I have no doubt." Again, Charlie scanned the chart. "Humor me. Stay. Live to walk your daughter down the aisle."

Yikes.

Bryce huffed his displeasure.

"Of course he'll stay." The look Celine gave Bryce said there'd be hell to pay if he disregarded his doctor's orders.

"I'll get out of your way." I edge toward the door.

"Thank you for the flowers," said Bryce. "They smell nice."

"I hope you enjoy them." I was a step closer to escape.

"Ellison, I'll be a few minutes, but I'd like a word. Would you please wait in the hall?"

"Of course. Bryce, feel better."

I stepped into the hallway, which was painted in a shade of over-cooked oatmeal, and waited for Charlie. Pacing. Thinking.

Libba and I should have shared our plan with Charlie. After all, Olivia was his ex-wife, and Bryce was his patient. And one trying to kill the other was undoubtedly awkward for him. Except…Bryce hadn't recognized Olivia. Which begged the question, how could she cause a heart attack in a man she'd never met?

"Where is she?" Charlie grabbed my arm.

"Who?"

"Libba."

"The coffee shop. She wanted to visit Bryce with me, but the nurse wouldn't let her in."

"Why visit Bryce?"

"To see if he recognized Olivia."

Charlie was a doctor. Surely he was smart enough to come up

with the same idea. But, what would he say? This is my ex-wife. I think she tried to kill you. Have you seen her before?

"Did he recognize her?"

"He did not. Maybe Olivia's innocent."

"Bryce failing to recognize her doesn't mean anything. She's sneaky."

Sneaky, Olivia might be, but she still needed access to her victims. How had she drugged or poisoned them without getting close to them?

"You don't look convinced. You should be. Remember, she tried to kill Libba and me last night."

"Speaking of, Libba is waiting for me in the coffee shop. Alone."

He raked his fingers through his short hair. "I have to finish rounds, or I'd join you."

I took a step toward the elevator.

"Ellison."

"What?"

"Is she okay?" The poor man looked bereft.

"Libba's fine. Come by the house for dinner tonight." I walked to the elevator and jabbed the button.

The doors opened, revealing John Abrams. He nodded at me. "Ellison."

I stepped into the car.

"Going down?" he asked.

"Yes."

"Lobby?"

"Please."

He pushed the button. But rather than get off the elevator, he watched the doors slide shut. "Visiting someone?"

"Bryce Fowler."

"I'm told he's improving. Good news."

"It is. Charlie says he can go home in a few days."

"Better news. I enjoyed chatting with you at dinner the other night." He winced. "I need to write your mother a note."

"She'd appreciate that." And she'd hold it against him if he didn't send a thank you note. I hoped Rick Lawson didn't send one.

He rubbed the tip of his nose. "I hope, when we were at dinner, that I didn't give the impression I take Charlie's patients ailments lightly. I don't. He's a good doctor."

"Not at all."

"Good. Good. Please, tell your sister I wish her luck with her new house."

We arrived at the lobby, and the doors opened.

"I will."

I stepped off the elevator. John did not.

When I turned to look at him, he grinned. "I have patients to see. Just wanted to chat for a minute."

"Well, it was nice talking to you."

The doors slid shut before I could say more.

I found Libba in the coffee shop, nursing a cup of tea.

I wrinkled my nose. "Brown water."

"Do we need to discuss your coffee addiction?"

The waitress, who knew me, brought me a cup without my having to ask for it. "Thank you."

"My pleasure, Mrs. Jones. Would you care for a slice of pie? We have your favorite."

"It's a bit early in the day, but thank you for offering."

When the waitress left, Libba speared me with her gaze. "Well?"

"Bryce didn't recognize her. I believed him."

"That means we need to talk to Elaine and Joanne."

"Not today."

"Why not?"

I don't want to wasn't a valid reason. At least not for Libba. "I have other things to do."

"More important than catching a killer?" She reached across

the table and caught my hand. "Please. The woman tried to murder me last night. We need to catch her."

"Some might argue we need to stay far away from her." Anarchy would argue that.

The waitress put my coffee on the table.

I thanked her, added cream, laced my fingers around the mug, and took a grateful sip.

"You look like an addict getting her fix."

"Stop." I was tired of Libba ribbing me over my love of coffee. "It's just coffee. Not liquor. Not diet pills. Not sleeping pills. Just. Coffee."

"Mrs. Jones?" The waitress had returned, and she looked nervous about interrupting us.

I looked up at her and smiled. She was an older woman with bubble-gum pink lipstick, a gravity-defying beehive, and kind eyes beneath blue-shadowed lids. "Yes?"

"I was standing near the entrance to the lobby and I heard on the PA system, someone is requesting that Ellison Russell check in with the front desk."

My stomach sank. Whatever called me to the front desk, it couldn't be good.

"Who knows we're here?" asked Libba.

"Aggie." I stood. Abruptly. "What if something happened to one of the kids?" I was out the coffee shop door and standing at the front desk before I knew I was moving. "I'm Ellison Jones. Ellison Russell. I mean, Jones."

"Mrs. Russell—"

"It's Jones."

The volunteer pulled on the collar of her smock. "Mrs. Jones, your mother asked us to locate you."

Mother? This was extreme, even for her. "Did she say what's wrong?"

"She asks that you join her in the emergency room. Your father has been admitted."

Thankful for my unerring knowledge of the hospital's corridors, I flew to the waiting room for the ER.

Mother wasn't there, and a line had formed to speak with the admitting nurse.

"Now what?" asked Libba, who'd followed me.

I pushed through the doors to the treatment rooms.

"Ma'am. The admitting nurse followed me. "You can't be in here."

"I'm Frances Walford's daughter."

"Oh." She took a step back. "My apologies. Please, go ahead."

For once, I didn't mind using Mother's name.

"Excuse me." I stopped a nurse. "I'm looking for Frances Walford."

"Last room on the right."

"Thank you." I hurried down the hallway with Libba at my heels.

As if she sensed my arrival, Mother stepped into the hallway. "Where have you been?"

"I came as soon as I heard. How's Dad?"

Mother's lower lip trembled.

In my entire life, had I ever seen my mother cry? I didn't think so. I opened my arms to hug her.

"No," she rasped. Then she held up her hands as if she were warding off evil. "No. Your father needs me to be strong."

Daddy wouldn't know if I hugged Mother, but I didn't argue. "What happened?"

Mother took a deep breath. She squared her shoulders. She lifted her chin. Only when her posture was perfect did she reply. "Your father is unconscious."

"What do the doctors say?"

"They think he had a heart attack." Her eyes welled, and she wrapped her arms around her torso, holding herself together. "They're…they're not hopeful."

CHAPTER THIRTEEN

I sat next to my father's bed, clutched his hand, and took stock of his room. They'd moved him from the emergency department hours ago, but this was my first opportunity to be with him. The mint-hued walls were an affront to colors everywhere. Who picked the paint colors for hospitals? Sadists? Blind men? A tired white blanket covered Daddy's bed. And I sat straight in a baby-poo-brown Naugahyde recliner. When I stood, the sound of my thighs pulling away from the chair's surface would be appalling.

Studying the room was so much better than looking at Daddy. My father was tall and strong and handsome with a shock of white hair and a deep golfer's tan. Except, he wasn't. Not now. The skin on his face draped his cheek bones loosely. The hospital lighting turned his hair a faded almost-sepia yellow. And his tan looked like jaundice.

Whenever I looked at him, my eyes filled.

"Daddy, wake up." I focused on the hospital blanket.

How could I go on without him? He was the man who'd encouraged me to attend art school. The man whose uncondi-tional love gave me strength. The man who softened Mother's hard edges and acted as peacekeeper. He couldn't die. Mother wouldn't allow it. I wouldn't allow it. I wasn't ready to let him go.

"Do you remember when Marjorie and I were little, and Mother put us in matching dresses for Easter? Marjorie hated that we matched, and she purposefully spilled juice in my lap right before we left for church."

Mother's annoyance had been palpable. With Marjorie. But also with me and my tears.

"You took me upstairs and helped me pick out another dress. You dried my tears. You promised that Marjorie didn't actually hate me. You made everything better. You were my rock."

I wiped my eyes. Could he even hear me?

"We called Marjorie. She's on a plane right now. She'll be here soon. Karma's in the waiting room with Grace and Beau. They'd be here with you, but the hospital is only allowing one visitor at a time."

"Frances?" Daddy's voice was barely a whisper.

He was conscious. I wanted to whoop and laugh and cry all at the same time. Instead, I tightened my grip on his hand. "I'm here, Daddy. Mother is in the chapel negotiating with God."

Daddy chuckled, then grimaced as if the tiny laugh had hurt his chest. "Where am I?"

"The hospital. You had a heart attack."

"Not possible."

Yet, here we were. "Well, that's what the doctors tell us."

"No. I saw a doctor on Friday." His tongue darted out and wet his dry lips.

"Are you thirsty?" I picked up a plastic cup in a sickly shade of mauve and bent the straw.

"Yes."

I held the cup while my father drank.

"Thank you."

"You're welcome."

"The doctor told me I was in good shape. Great shape for a man my age."

I wasn't going to argue with a man in a hospital bed. One who looked exhausted. "When you went to the doctor, who did you see?"

"Charlie."

I put the cup on the table near the bed and sat back in my chair. How had Olivia gotten to Daddy? My father wasn't the kind of man who'd cheat on his wife. Also, he adored my mother. He didn't even look at other women. There was no easy opportunity for her to get close to him. "Was that the first time you saw him? As a patient, I mean."

"Yes."

I closed my eyes and thought. Hard.

"Ellison." I hated the weakness in his voice.

"What, Daddy?"

He rubbed his chest. "We need to talk about Beau."

I stiffened. "Why?"

"We may not get another chance."

"Don't talk like that. You'll be fine."

"We need to talk." In his own way, Daddy could be as intransigent as Mother.

"What about Beau?"

He stared into my eyes. "Are you sure about that boy?"

"About making him a part of our family? Absolutely."

"Your mother has reservations."

It wasn't her concern. "She'll get over them."

His lips curled in an attempt at a smile. "You sure about that?"

"She accepted Karma."

Daddy winced. "You've gotten more direct this past year."

Finding countless bodies and falling in love with a man like Anarchy did that for a woman.

"I'm proud of you, Ellison."

"Don't say that." It sounded too much like goodbye.

"I'm not proud of you?"

"You can be proud of me, but tell me when we're having cocktails at the club."

"You need to know."

"You're going to get better." If only his skin tone wasn't so awful.

Daddy shivered.

"I can ask the nurse for a warm blanket."

I stood and the separation of my skin from the Naugahyde sounded like a trumpet of flatulence.

"Don't leave." He flushed, realizing how desperate he sounded. "There should be a call button." He fumbled with a cord, searching for the box at the end.

I took it from his hands and pressed the button.

"Harrington?" Mother stood at the entrance to Daddy's room. "You're awake."

For an instant, they simply stared at each other.

Mother's usually firm chin wobbled.

Daddy's eyes watered.

Then, he said, "Frannie." Her name on his lips was both a prayer and a promise.

She rushed to his bedside, and they held each other.

A brave nurse entered Daddy's room, counted noses, and said, "I'm so sorry, Mrs. Walford, but one of you will have to leave."

Mother scowled at her, and the nurse's bravery faltered. She retreated a step.

"I'll go." Mother and Daddy needed time alone.

I bent and kissed my father's cheek.

"Love you, Ellie."

"Love you too, Daddy."

As I was leaving, the nurse said, "You rang for help?"

"May I please have a warm blanket?" Daddy already sounded stronger, as if Mother was a tonic.

I paused in the hallway, giving myself a moment to process the emotions pinballing through me. I would not cry. I would not cry. Tears wet my face.

"Darn it." I rooted through my handbag for a handkerchief.

"Need this?" Anarchy held out a neatly folded linen square.

I launched myself into his arms. "You're here."

His lips pressed against my temple. "I'm sorry I didn't arrive sooner. How is he?"

My throat tightened, and fresh tears ran down my cheeks.

He held me closer, and I melted into him.

If Mother stepped into the hallway, she'd be scandalized. I didn't much care.

"He's awake."

Anarchy reclaimed his handkerchief and dried my tears. "That's good news."

I nodded.

"Who's his doctor?"

"Charlie."

Anarchy stiffened.

"When Daddy is feeling better, we can ask about Olivia." My father would get better. There was no other option. "His first visit with Charlie was Friday."

"You don't think Olivia's involved?" It was as if Anarchy had read my mind.

"I think she's nuts and angry and vengeful. But the woman who tried to crush her ex-husband and his girlfriend between two cars in a moment of pique...is she the same woman who carefully plans multiple murders?"

"Then who?"

"Rick Lawson."

"The doctor? The one who was at dinner Sunday night?"

"That's the one."

"Doctors swear an oath to heal."

I stared at him.

"Okay, Okay. That sounded like Pollyanna. But why would he go after Charlie's patients?"

"He wants to be head of the department? Rick could have put something in Daddy's drink on Sunday night. Something slow acting."

"We would have noticed."

"Not if he did it during the fire. Just think about it."

"I will. In the meantime, what can we do for your dad?"

"Pray."

Together, we walked to the waiting room and found Karma sitting by herself.

"How is he?" She rose from her chair.

"Awake. Talking to Mother."

"Thank heavens."

"Where are the kids?"

"Libba took them for pie."

"The coffee shop has great pie." John Abrams entered the waiting room and gave me an awkward pat on the shoulder. "I just heard." He extended his hand to my husband, and they shook. Then, his gaze shifted to Karma. "How is he?"

"Ellison says he's awake."

John nodded. "Good news. Do you know what happened?"

"Mother says he collapsed shortly after breakfast. She called an ambulance while the man who helps with the yard started CPR."

"Charlie's his doctor?"

"Yes."

"Excellent. Your father's in good hands. What can I do for you and your family?"

"Nothing, right now, but thank you for offering."

"Of course." He glanced at his watch. "I have to get back to my office, but you'll let me know if you need me?"

"We will. Thank you."

John left us, and Karma waited a few seconds before saying, "He's a nice man."

"Too bad about the comb-over."

"Ellison!"

"What? Hunter has great hair."

My sister blushed.

I glanced at my watch. "I should phone Aggie. Marjorie said she'd call with her flight information."

"When you're done, we'll get you some coffee." Anarchy really was the perfect man.

I made my way to the payphones, dropped a dime in the slot, and dialed home.

"Jones' residence."

"Aggie, it's me."

"How's your father?"

"Awake. I'm hopeful. Did Marjorie call?"

"Her flight lands at six. She asked me to prepare the blue room."

Oh dear Lord. Karma was in the blue room. In fact, all my guest rooms were full. "What did you tell her?" Unless Marjorie deigned to stay in the apartment above the garage, I didn't have space for her.

"I explained all your bedrooms were occupied."

"How did she take it?"

"Not well." Those two small words spoke volumes.

"She can have the carriage house, or she can stay with Mother."

"She mentioned something about the Alameda."

A hotel was a solid third option.

"I'm sorry you had to deal with her." Marjorie, when she didn't get her way, was not pleasant.

"You have enough on your plate."

"Thank you, Aggie. For everything." My eyes welled. It was as if a need to cry lurked just beneath my skin.

"You're welcome. Will you be home for dinner?"

"I'm not sure."

"I understand. I'll make chicken salad and put it in the fridge. Will you please keep me posted?"

"Of course."

We hung up, and I returned to the waiting room.

"Do I need to leave for the airport?" asked Anarchy.

"No. She doesn't land until six."

"Then come with me." He claimed my hand. "You need coffee. Karma, do you want to join us?"

"I think I'll stay. If Frances steps out, someone should be here."

More tears threatened. I swallowed them. "Can we get you anything?"

"Tab, if they have it."

Anarchy led me to the elevator and pushed the down button. "How's Frances?"

"She relies on him, more than she lets on. I'm glad I was here when they brought him in. Mother needed me."

He frowned. "You were already here?"

Anarchy would not like my answer. "I visited Bryce. In case you're wondering, he didn't recognize Olivia."

"Ellison!"

"What? Is there an investigation?"

"No," he admitted.

"Then I wasn't interfering in an investigation."

"You really think she's innocent?"

"I already told you. She might have a motive, but where's the opportunity?"

"An accomplice?"

"She comes to town and finds someone to help her kill the city's scions?"

"You're right. No accomplice."

The elevator door slid open, and we hurried to the coffee shop.

Libba and the kids sat at a table near the window. Grace rose from her chair when she saw us.

"He's awake," I told her. "You can see him later. Eat your pie." A slice of apple à la mode waited at her place.

Anarchy pulled out a chair, and I sat. "Beau, is that French silk?"

"It's my favorite."

I'd be sure and tell Aggie.

WE GATHERED FOR SUPPER AT OUR HOUSE—GRACE, BEAU, Karma, Libba, Charlie, Anarchy and me.

Mother and Marjorie remained at the hospital. For which I was eternally grateful.

When the last plate was cleared, Grace said, "Can Beau and I take the dogs for a walk?"

"Yes, please." Sometimes, when she rolled her eyes or gave me attitude, I wondered about my life choices. Other times, like tonight, I realized I had the best kid in the world.

The kids and dogs left, and I said, "Shall we sit on the patio?"

"It's hot out," said Libba.

"The patio is shaded, and I spent all day indoors. I could use some fresh air."

"Fine," she ceded. "But I need more wine."

We grabbed a bottle on our way outside, then gathered around the wrought-iron table.

Charlie sank deep into his chair and took a sip of his bourbon. "Ellison, I'm so sorry."

"For what?"

"Olivia. This is my fault."

"If Olivia did this, it's her fault, not yours. Also, I don't think she did it."

"Of course she did. You were there last night. You saved us when she tried to run us down." He reached for Libba's hand.

"Trying to squash you doesn't mean she's poisoning your patients."

"Of course it does."

"Charlie, you told me she wanted to ruin you. Destroy your reputation. Take your kids. Destroy your life."

He nodded. "You're making the case for me."

"If I planned on destroying someone, I wouldn't tell them. I'd put my plan in motion, ruin their life, and only when they hit bottom would I tell them I was responsible."

Anarchy grinned at me. "That's a bit terrifying, sweetheart. Remind me never to cross you."

"If. If I planned. I never would."

"What's your point, Ellison?"

"Olivia seems like a woman who's emotionally reactive. You file for divorce, she threatens you. You kiss Libba, she tries to ram you with a car. This long game? I don't see it."

"You don't know her."

"True. But what if it's someone else?"

"Like who?"

"Rick Lawson."

"Impossible." Charlie shook his head. Vehemently.

"That was my knee-jerk reaction as well," said Anarchy. "Then I considered Ellison's theory. If you leave the hospital, who would head the department?"

Charlie shook his head.

"If we accept these heart attacks aren't natural, then we need to look for motive. Seems to me that Rick has a good one."

"He's a doctor. He would never cause harm."

It was pure Pollyanna when Anarchy said it. The same for Charlie.

"Don't be naïve. Doctors can kill."

"It has to be Olivia." Ostrich head meet sand.

"Why, Charlie?"

He glared at me.

If Olivia was a killer, he'd get full custody of his children, she'd be out of his life, and her threats would be meaningless. And maybe, just maybe, he wanted to see the woman who'd put him through a hellish divorce trade in her orange Hermès bag for an orange jumpsuit.

"It's not Rick. We're friends."

I mentally reviewed the things Rick had said about Charlie just this morning. "I don't think you are."

Charlie pushed out of his chair so abruptly that he nearly knocked it over. Then he turned his back on me and stalked across our backyard to his own.

"Well," said Libba. "That went swimmingly."

"I'm sorry."

"Don't be. Everything you said makes sense. He's just not ready to hear it." She stood.

"Are you headed to bed?"

"Yes, but not here." She claimed the full wine bottle, then followed Charlie home.

"He'll come around," said Anarchy.

I hoped so. "I truly don't think she killed those men."

"I agree with you. What do we know about Rick Lawson?"

"He's forty-seven, twice divorced, and has a good reputation as a physician."

"Money problems?"

"I don't know. If he's writing two alimony checks, it's possible."

"I'll have Peters check him out." Anarchy studied my face. "You're tired."

It was barely nine o'clock, but I stifled a yawn. "Long day."

"Let's get you to bed."

I wasn't about to argue.

"Mom!" Grace stood at the back door. The way she held onto the door frame, the pitch of her voice, something was wrong.

I stood. "What is it, honey? Where's Beau?"

"I'm here." He joined Grace in the doorway. "Someone followed us. On our walk."

"Who? Are you hurt?"

"We're fine," said Grace.

"Description?" Anarchy used his cop voice.

"It was a woman," Grace replied.

"She was pretty and blonde," Beau added. "And she gave me the creeps."

"What happened?"

"She tried to grab Beau, and Max lunged for her. I thought he might rip her throat out. Then, she ran away."

I loved my dog.

CHAPTER FOURTEEN

"The last few days have been absolutely dreadful," I told Mr. Coffee.

He gave a sympathetic gurgle.

Outside, the eastern sky was still a saturated shade of purple. It was too early for the sun. Too early for people. The house was still quiet, and Mr. Coffee and I had the kitchen to ourselves. Mostly. Max napped on the mat in the corner.

I took a coffee mug from the cabinet. "I say that, but I should be grateful. Beau and Grace are safe. When I think what could have happened…" Visions of what Olivia might have done to Beau had kept me up half the night.

They're safe now. Unhurt. They might even feel empowered. They did solve a problem without you.

I filled the mug to the brim and had to take a sip before I added cream. "Thanks to Max."

The dog—the hero—wagged his stubby tail as if, even in sleep, he knew we were praising him.

"I came too close to losing Beau. Maybe losing Grace, too."

You don't know that.

"I have to do better." I should have considered that Olivia might come after me. Or my family.

You're doing the best you can. Don't be so hard on yourself.

On that, we could agree to disagree. I settled on a stool at the island. "If Charlie had been here when the kids got home, he'd have said, 'I told you so.'"

Oh?

"He thinks his ex-wife is the devil incarnate."

What do you think?

I still didn't see how she could have killed those men. I gave a frustrated sigh.

Let's talk about something else.

"Marjorie is furious with me."

I hate to say it, but that's your sister's default state. Mr. Coffee wasn't wrong. She'd get over it. Eventually.

I took another sip of coffee. I needed it. "I've been meaning to call Hunter about a family lawyer, and I haven't found the time."

You've been busy.

"I wanted to swim this morning." Exercise usually cleared my mind, and my mind desperately needed clearing. "But Anarchy asked me not to go alone." Now, I was just whining.

Mr. Coffee didn't judge. *He cares about you. And, I have to say, I agree with him.*

I didn't agree, but I did understand. Olivia was a threat.

"My father nearly died, and he's still in the hospital." And would be for the foreseeable future.

But he's stable. On the mend.

"The police refuse to open an investigation into Charlie's patients' deaths." Anarchy had practically begged. "What if more people die before we can identify the killer?" My tales of woe were endless.

Ellison, you're not killing those men. It's not your fault.

I tightened my fingers around my mug, then lowered my

nose and breathed in the coffee aroma. Just its scent was a comfort. "We need to stop the killer."

Do you hear yourself? You said 'we.' Not that long ago you were alone. Now, you and Anarchy are a team.

"You always say exactly the right thing."

"Who are you talking to?" Beau had snuck down the back stairs without me noticing.

"How are you this morning?" I offered him a smile. "You're up early."

The sky was still a deep lavender. No sun in sight.

Beau looked around the kitchen as if he expected to see Anarchy or Aggie. "Were you talking to Max?"

"No," I admitted. "May I get you anything? A glass of milk? Juice?"

He shook his head, still puzzled by the empty kitchen. "If not Max, who?"

I flushed. "Mr. Coffee."

"It sounded as if you were having a real conversation."

Because we were. "You know that little voice in your head? Mr. Coffee is one of mine."

His eyes widened. "You have voices in your head?" Crazy people had voices in their heads.

"I have two." The psychology professor I had in college would say I had three, but I wasn't about to explain the id to Beau.

He swallowed. Audibly. "What do you mean?"

"I have a voice that points out my failures. It reminds me I'm not good enough, or smart enough, or strong enough. It tells me I should feel guilty or ashamed. Mr. Coffee? He does the opposite."

Beau stared at me. Steadily. As if he was waiting for a better explanation.

"For example, the negative voice in my head told me I did a terrible job taking care of you last night. I was irresponsible. I should have gone with you. I'm not a good mother. Mr. Coffee told me that you and Grace don't need a mom who hovers. You had Max and Finn to keep you safe."

"Finn just wagged his butt."

I couldn't help but smile. "Okay. You had Max there to keep you safe."

Max lifted his head, opened his amber eyes, wagged his stubby tail, and gazed soulfully at the treat jar on top of the refrigerator. Surely, his incredible heroics deserved additional treats.

"Or, that not-so-nice voice might tell me I'm a bad sister because Marjorie is staying in a hotel. Mr. Coffee might respond that she could easily stay with Mother, and I'm not responsible for her choices."

That Mr. Coffee is a smart guy. You should listen to him.

"What if the voice tells me I'm a bad swimmer? That I should just give up."

"I've seen you win races."

"But I'm not getting any better." Beau jammed his hands in his pajama pockets. "I'm getting slower. I'm getting worse."

The fault, dear Beau, lay not in your swimming, but with your coaches.

"Mr. Coffee might say he knows how hard you try. He might say you're too determined and strong to give up on something you enjoy. He might also say that you need to work with a better coach. One who can adjust your technique."

He knelt next to Max and stroked the dog's silken ears. "And if the voice says I was a bad son?"

My heart broke. Shattered. The coffee mug froze halfway to my lips, and it took everything I had to keep my voice steady. "Why would the voice say that?"

Beau avoided my gaze, staring at Aggie's spotless floors instead. "My dad didn't like me, and my mom didn't care about me."

Mr. Coffee would say scalding their nether regions with boiling coffee was too good for them.

"Mr. Coffee would say that becoming an adult doesn't make people smart. Your parents were stupid." About so many things. "You weren't a bad son. The opposite. They were bad parents."

He kept his gaze on the floor. I hadn't convinced him.

"If Anarchy or I did something bad, would it be Grace's fault?"

"No." He sounded positively outraged and speared me with an indignant scowl.

"So why are your parents' actions your fault?"

He blinked. Twice. Then he returned his gaze to Aggie's floors. "They didn't love me." His voice was so tiny, if I weren't paying close attention, I would have missed his words. He wiped the back of his hand across his eyes.

Would he shake off a hug? I sensed he wanted to be heard, not coddled. "Your parents were selfish people. They had the most amazing boy in the world living with them, and they were too wrapped up in their own drama to realize it."

"Grace is so lucky." His voice sounded wet, choked with unshed tears. "A minute ago..." he screwed his eyes closed, and his hand on Max's head stilled.

I waited.

Max nudged him for more pets.

"A minute ago, you said Grace and I don't need a mom who hovers."

"That's true." Did he *want* me to hover?

He stared a hole through the floor. "You think of yourself as my mom?"

"I do."

He jerked his head up and gazed at me with damp eyes. "You mean it?" Suspicion laced his voice.

"I do. I love you."

Beau jumped from the floor and rushed me. His hug nearly knocked me flat.

"Oomph." My arms tightened around him. "If you want, Anarchy and I can talk to a lawyer about making it official."

"What does that mean?"

I should have waited for Anarchy to have this conversation, but it was too late now. Beau needed to know how much we loved him. "We'd like to adopt you."

He stiffened inside the circle of my arms. "So I'd be Beau Jones?"

"If you like, or you could keep Riley. But Anarchy and I would be your parents. No matter what you decide, you'll always have a home with us and you'll always be loved. Nothing will ever change that."

"Anarchy agrees?"

"Anarchy adores you. Nothing would make him prouder than to have you as his son."

Beau's eyes welled, and tears ran down his cheeks. "Please," he said. "Talk to the lawyer."

"We'll call today."

"Wait. Is Grace okay with this?"

"Grace will be furious if we don't adopt you." I wiped a stray tear from my cheek. "We should celebrate."

"Celebrate?"

"I have just the thing." I let go of Beau (hard to do), went to the fridge, and took out a bottle of sparkling cider.

Woof! As long as I was standing next to the treats, would I give him one?

"Since we're celebrating." I grabbed a biscuit and gave it to Max.

He devoured it in seconds.

"We need glasses." I stepped into the butler's pantry and took two champagne flutes from the cabinet.

When I returned to the kitchen, Anarchy stood next to the

island with his arm draped around Beau's shoulders. His brown eyes shimmered with emotion.

"We need another glass," I said. "Two more. If we leave Grace out of this celebration, she'll never forgive us."

"I'll get her." Beau took off running.

I waited until his footsteps receded, then told Anarchy, "I'm sorry. It's a conversation we should have had together, but..." Another tear wet my cheek.

"But?"

"He's been through so much, and he deserves so much love. I didn't want him to wait another second to know how we feel."

Anarchy pulled me into his arms. "I'm just glad he said 'yes.'"

I DRESSED TO SPEND THE DAY AT THE HOSPITAL—KHAKI SLACKS, a white linen camp shirt, and a lightweight navy-blue cardigan thrown over my shoulders. I wore pearls at my neck and ears. I glanced in the mirror hung above my dresser. The outfit was unobjectionable. My make-up was subtle. My hair was neat. Mother would not be able to find fault. Important, because I had a feeling Mother would be about as pleasant as a bear awakened from hibernation.

I picked up the bottle of Cristalle that Anarchy bought me on our honeymoon and spritzed the delicate floral scent behind my ears. When I returned the simple, elegant Chanel bottle to the silver tray that held my perfumes, I noticed Bryce's pills.

My hand hovered above the medication.

How could I have been so blind?

I snatched up the bottle and hurried to the kitchen.

"Good morning." Aggie's greeting was as bright as she was, which was saying something given her daffodil yellow kaftan. "How's your father?"

"I talked to Mother a little while ago." She'd been surly. "He slept poorly last night and wants to go home."

"Men are seldom good patients."

True. "Are you using the island for anything?"

"No. Why?"

I carefully poured Bryce's pills onto the clean surface.

Aggie lifted her brows.

"Would you please help me?"

She nodded. "With what?"

"I want to see if they're all the same."

We studied each pill. Tiny white ovals marked with the letters NG.

The first ten were identical.

The eleventh was different. Slightly larger. No NG.

If I wasn't looking, I wouldn't have noticed. "Someone tampered with Bryce's pills."

"His wife?" Aggie asked a legitimate question.

I picked up the bottle and studied the label. "I don't think so. More likely, the pharmacist."

"Where was the prescription filled?"

"The hospital pharmacy." I crossed the kitchen to the phone. "I need to tell Anarchy."

Brnng, brnng.

I snatched the receiver from the cradle. "Jones' residence."

"Ellison? It's Jinx. I'm calling to ask after your father."

Which was nice of her, but I had a call to make. "He's ready to go home. His doctors don't agree."

"Frances will keep him in line."

As long as I had her on the phone… "Jinx, what pharmacy do you use?"

"Bruce Smith on the Plaza. Why?"

"And George?"

"On the rare occasion George actually goes to the doctor, he has his prescriptions filled at the hospital pharmacy. He says he doesn't have to wait in line while ladies buy lipsticks." Bruce Smith carried an impressive array of drugstore make-up. "Why do you ask?" Jinx's gossip radar was undoubtedly beeping madly.

"I have an idea. If I'm right, I'll tell you all about it."

"Is this about Charlie's patients?" There were no flies on Jinx.

"I—"

"It's okay, Ellison. Even if you're wrong, you'll tell me."

"I promise."

We chatted for a few more minutes—minutes that seemed to last forever—then hung up.

I immediately called Anarchy.

"Jones."

"It's me."

"Is your dad okay?" Concern laced his tone.

"I think so." I took a breath. "I know how they did it."

"Who did what?"

"The killer. I know how he killed those men. He mixed their medications. Maybe the extra pills cause heart attacks. Or maybe they're a drug that shouldn't be taken with heart medication. Either way, the pharmacist put pills that shouldn't be there into the prescription bottle."

"How do you know?"

"I accidentally came home with Bryce's medication." I glanced at the island and Aggie held up her hand spread wide. Five. Five pills that shouldn't be there. "I bet, if we check, we'll find that Owen and Lee used the same pharmacy as Bryce."

"I'll check." He was silent for a few seconds. "Not Olivia."

"No," I agreed. "Not Olivia."

"We're still looking for her."

The worry I'd felt for our children had morphed into anger. She might not have hurt them, but she'd scared them half to death. And me, too. "Good." The woman deserved to be in jail.

"Are you headed to the hospital?"

"I am."

"I'll tell my captain about the pills, then reach out to Elaine Sandingham and Joanne Woodfield."

I pinched the bridge of my nose. "I know the how, but I still don't understand why. Why would a pharmacist do this?"

"Which pharmacy?"

"The one at the hospital."

"Ellison—"

"I know. I know. I'll stay away from the pharmacy. You have my word."

"Please, be careful."

"Karma, Marjorie, and I will spend most of our day in the waiting room." Add in Mother and Daddy in a grumpy mood and it promised to be a laugh riot.

"Will you tell your mother?" He meant about Beau, not the pharmacy. Although, as the hospital board president, someone should probably tell her that the hospital pharmacy was killing patients.

"Not today." Marjorie would weigh in, and her opinion would not be helpful.

"I want you to check in with me every hour."

"Anarchy—"

"I mean it, Ellison. There's a killer in that hospital, and we both know you have a habit of attracting trouble."

CHAPTER FIFTEEN

I f I never saw over-cooked oatmeal walls again, it would be too soon. I shifted in my chair, trying to find a comfortable position.

From across the waiting room, Marjorie glared at me. She hadn't stopped glaring for four hours.

"Just say it." I was tired of her scowls.

"I can't believe you had me fly across the country in a panic."

"Marjorie, we thought he might die. Would you prefer we hadn't called you?"

She muttered something about boys and cries and wolves.

I lowered my gaze and flipped through the magazine I'd bought at the gift shop. Any reply I made would only make her angrier.

"You gave her my bedroom." She positively seethed.

Oh dear Lord. "Marjorie, I didn't *give* her your room. Karma bought a house. She's just staying with me, in *my* guest room, until the closing."

"Why didn't she stay with Mother and Daddy?"

"For three weeks?"

She couldn't be serious. Marjorie was here for a few days, and rather than stay with our parents, she'd booked herself into a hotel. "It's ridiculous how the whole family caters to her. Mother even hosted a dinner party for her."

Jealous. Marjorie was jealous.

I was wise enough not to point that out. "You heard about that?"

"People from New York to San Francisco have heard about that." Her lips twitched. "It's not every day the chef at the country club sets himself on fire over bananas Foster."

"Cherries jubilee."

"Potato. Potahto."

"It was a memorable evening."

Her lips twitched again. "I wish I could have been there." Then her scowl returned, as if she realized she'd almost done the unthinkable, and smiled at me. She glanced at her watch. "Where is she? It's my turn."

In deference to Mother, the hospital was now allowing two visitors in Daddy's room. Karma, Marjorie, and I were rotating.

"She's only a few minutes late."

Marjorie collected her handbag and her righteous indignation. "You need to decide whose side you're on."

"There are no sides, Marjorie."

"Don't be naïve. She's stealing my family."

Wow. Just wow. "Karma is not taking your place. You're just feeling…insecure."

"Save your drugstore psychology." She stalked off.

I lowered my head to my hands, barely moving when Karma dropped into the chair next to mine.

"I don't know about you, but I could use a cup of coffee." She'd uttered the magic words.

I lifted my forehead from my palms. "Lots of fun in there?"

"Your mother is in rare form. Every nurse on the floor is terrified."

That didn't surprise me. "Marjorie's no picnic either."

"She doesn't speak to me." She should count herself lucky.

"Coffee shop?" I asked. "Pie?"

Karma's eyes flared with interest. "Let's!"

We took the elevator to the crowded lobby.

"Busy today," Karma observed.

I didn't answer. I was too busy staring at an orange Hermès bag. "Karma." I grabbed her forearm. "Look there. By the revolving door."

"What am I looking at?"

"The blonde with the orange handbag. It's Olivia."

Had I been wrong? Had Olivia seduced a pharmacist into killing Charlie's patients? Maybe she'd paid him. "Keep an eye on her. I'll call Anarchy."

I hurried to the wall of pay phones.

Why would Olivia risk coming to the place where Charlie worked? It made no sense. Unless she figured this was the last place we'd look for her.

The phones were all engaged, and I tapped an impatient hand against my thigh. Long seconds passed, and I searched the lobby for Olivia.

She really was pretty.

Several men were openly staring. As I watched, a man approached her, leaned forward, and kissed her cheek.

She smiled up at him.

Someone tapped me on the shoulder, and I jumped, then pressed my palm to my heart.

"I'm sorry," said the woman who'd tapped me. "I'm done with the phone, and I thought you were waiting."

"I am. Thank you."

I dropped a dime in the slot and called Anarchy.

"Jones."

"I'm in the hospital lobby. So is Olivia."

"What?" Anarchy's surprise and concern carried through the

phone line. "Don't go near her."

"I won't." I hunched over the receiver and whispered, "Rick Lawson just kissed her."

"Do they know you've spotted them?"

"No." I glanced over my shoulder. Both Olivia and Rick were looking right at me. Their combined gazes felt like a hundred spiders. A thousand spiders. Or a single slithery snake. I shuddered. "Yes."

"Are you alone?" Anarchy's voice was cool and analytical. He'd switched to cop mode.

"Karma's here somewhere, and there are lots of people in the lobby."

"A security guard?"

"I don't see one."

"When you hang up the phone, go to the front desk and tell them you want a guard to escort you to your dad's room."

"Anarchy—"

"Do it, Ellison."

"But—"

"Use your mother's name. Whatever it takes. Promise me."

"But—"

"Please, Ellison. We don't know what she'll do. Please."

"Fine."

"I'm on my way. I'll see you in Harrington's room."

I did as Anarchy asked. I approached the busy front desk and smiled at the woman who sat on the other side. "Would you please call security?"

The woman, who had a tight perm and a tighter set to her lips, regarded me with mild interest. "What's the problem, ma'am?"

Inwardly, I cringed. "I need a security guard to escort me to my father's room."

"That's not why we have security, ma'am."

"I know, but this is a special case." Did I tell her there was a killer in the lobby? She looked like the sort who might scream. "I'm Frances Walford's daughter. I have an issue, and I want a security guard to escort me upstairs."

"Is there a problem, Gladys?"

I stiffened as if a snake had just circled my ankles.

Rick Lawson stood next to me.

"This lady is requesting a security guard," Gladys replied.

"Is she?" Rick looked amused. "Where are you going, Ellison? I'll be happy to escort you."

"No, thank you." My heart beat double time. I looked at Gladys and managed a tight smile. "My husband is a homicide detective. He's concerned for my safety. Please call a guard."

Out of the corner of my eyes, I saw Rick tap his temple.

"I am not crazy." I kept my voice calm and steady, a miracle given the adrenalin flooding my system. "If you can't call a guard for me, I'll wait here until my husband arrives."

A line was forming behind me.

"Ellison, be reasonable." Rick took hold of my arm. "I'll take you to your father's room. We can talk on the way."

"Don't touch me."

"You're hysterical."

I wasn't. I felt nothing but calm certainty. If I left the lobby with Rick, I'd never make it to my father's room.

"People are waiting, ma'am." Gladys leaned in her chair and peered around me at the growing line.

Guilt nipped at me. Those people had loved ones to check on. I was keeping them from their days. I steeled my resolve. "Then call for a guard."

Rick flashed Gladys a charming grin. "She doesn't need a guard. I'll take care of her."

I rested my hands on the desk, hating what I was about to do. "Gladys, my mother is Frances Walford. She is the chairman of the board at this hospital." I glanced at Rick. "Numerous people are about to lose their jobs. Do you want to be one of them?"

"I'm a volunteer." Did she think that would save her?

"You won't be if Mother hears about this."

Gladys paled.

"Please, Gladys, call the guard."

"Don't make that call, Gladys."

Gladys shook her head. "I'm sorry, Dr. Lawson. I think I'd better call."

Rick scowled at me, then melted into the crowd.

"If you'll step aside, ma'am?"

"I'll stay right here until you call." My insides churned with incipient nausea. People should treat each other as they'd like to be treated. I hated behaving like this. I'd hate being a murder victim even more.

Gladys phoned security, and in the snidest of tones, explained what I needed. Then she grinned at me. "They're too busy."

"Give me the phone." I held out my hand. "Please."

For a few seconds, Gladys looked as if she might refuse, then she slapped the receiver into my palm.

I angled myself away from Gladys, half-covered the receiver with a cupped palm, and spoke in low tones. "My name is Ellison Jones. I am Frances Walford's daughter, and I am married to Detective Anarchy Jones. He's a homicide detective. I recognized a killer in the hospital lobby. As a professional courtesy, my husband requests that someone, preferably someone who carries a firearm, return me safely to my father's room. My husband is on his way to the hospital right now, and he expects to find me alive and unharmed when he arrives."

There was a few seconds of silence, then a man said, "We're sending someone immediately, Mrs. Jones."

"Thank you." I returned the phone to Gladys. I didn't gloat. Gloating was beneath me. But, Lord, I wanted to.

"Ellison." Karma joined me in front of the desk. "What are you doing here? I thought you were calling Anarchy."

"I did. He wants us to have a guard."

She stepped closer. "I kept watch. Olivia just left with Rick Lawson."

I drew a breath deep into my lungs, then exhaled slowly.

"Do you think they're in cahoots?"

Cahoots. "It looks that way." And Mother needed to know.

"What's wrong?" she asked.

"Why do you think something's wrong?"

"The expression on your face. A lemon pucker mixed with smelling rotten eggs."

That made sense. "I have to tell Mother."

"Mrs. Jones?" A man the size of a rhinoceros held out his hand. "I'm Sid, your escort."

His hand swallowed mine.

"Thank you for coming."

"Let's get you to your father's room."

We reached Daddy's floor, and Sid agreed to stay with Karma until Anarchy arrived.

I stuck my head in his room and said, "Marjorie, I need to speak with Mother."

"It's not your turn."

Mother gave a why-can't-you-girls-get-along sigh. "Can it wait, Ellison?"

"No," I replied. "It cannot. It's about Charlie's patients."

Mother pursed her lips. "Marjorie, would you please give us a few minutes?"

With poor grace, Marjorie collected her handbag and stomped out of the room.

"She's already annoyed with you," Mother observed.

"Too bad." We had bigger problems than Marjorie's temper.

Mother rose from her chair. "What do you know about Charlie's patients?"

"Daddy, did Charlie write you a prescription when you saw him last week?"

"He did."

"Where did you have it filled?"

"Here."

"Ellison." Mother frowned at me as if I were wasting her time. "What's this about?"

"You'd better sit down."

She lifted her chin and remained standing.

"Someone in the hospital pharmacy has been putting the wrong pills in medication bottles. Specifically pills prescribed to Charlie's patients."

"What do you mean?"

"Are you sure you won't sit down?"

"Ellison, explain."

"I accidentally came home with a bottle of Bryce's heart medication. There were two different pills in the bottle. One of them almost killed him."

We both looked at Daddy, then she shook her head, disbelieving. "You're suggesting a pharmacist holds a grudge against Charlie and decided to kill his patients?"

"No. A doctor. One who was passed over for the head of the department."

Mother sat.

A minute passed. Then another. Her face remained impassive. "This could ruin the department—the hospital. Who?"

The door to Daddy's room swung open. "It's been more than a few minutes." The look on Marjorie's face said she hoped I'd argue.

"We're not done talking."

Mother, who looked unnaturally pale, held up a manicured hand. "It's all right, Ellison. I need a few minutes." Mother never needed time.

I'd sent her reeling. "I'll be in the waiting room. Anarchy's on his way. We can talk more when he gets here."

Mother's answering nod was grim.

I stepped into the hallway and almost bumped into John Abrams. "I'm sorry." I retreated a step.

"How's the patient?"

"Better." It was true. Daddy looked tanned rather than jaundiced.

"I need to explain something to you."

I glanced down the hallway, where Karma and Sid stood just outside the waiting room. "Explain what?" Had John known about Rick?

"In here." He pulled me into a vacant room.

"John, I promised Anarchy I'd stay in my father's room or with a guard."

"Smart." He pulled a syringe from the pocket of his lab coat. "I heard you talking to your mother just now."

Oh dear Lord. Right theory, wrong doctor. Ice ran through my veins.

I edged toward the door, but John blocked my path.

"Why kill those men?"

"I didn't kill them. Their medication was muddled."

"Is that what the pharmacist will say?"

"The pharmacist took an unfortunate tumble down a flight of stairs last night. His neck was broken." John shrugged. "No great loss. The man was a greedy bastard."

"You're a doctor!" And apparently I'd caught the Pollyanna bug, believing that doctors were above murder.

"I should be the head of this department. I have seniority. My patients love me. I save lives." The man believed he was God.

"And you take them."

"When I'm head, I'll make changes. We'll save more patients, have better outcomes."

I groaned. How could I have been so wrong? "I thought it was Rick."

"Rick? I should be offended. He's too busy chasing nurses to put together a plan like mine." A satisfied expression settled on

John's face. "How perfect that's he's been sleeping with Charlie's ex. It makes him look guilty as sin." John tapped the syringe, and a tiny drop of liquid gathered at the tip of the needle.

I retreated until the back of my legs pressed against the empty hospital bed.

My mouth was dry as dust, my fingers were chilled, and my legs were ready to run. But first, I needed a clear path to the door. With John and his poison blocking the way, escape didn't seem likely.

I reached behind my back where a tub of supplies waited for the bed's next occupant. My fingers closed around something cool and metal.

John took a step closer. "It won't hurt. I promise."

I tightened my grip and swung.

The bedpan meeting John's face made a gong-like sound, and he stumbled backward. I jerked my knee upward into the apex of his legs and took vicious delight in his gasp of pain.

He bent over, and I lifted the bedpan high above my head before slamming it into his skull.

The gong was louder the second time.

Then, I ran. I burst into the hallway and screamed, "Sid!"

The security guard raced toward me, his steps loud enough to reverberate through the hallway.

Mother opened the door to Daddy's room. "Ellison, why on earth are you yelling? In a hospital!" She was positively scandalized.

I ignored her and pointed Sid to the room where John had tried to kill me. "In there."

He pushed open the door.

Almost nothing had changed.

John was still on the floor.

A dented bedpan still lay next to him.

But the syringe, the one he'd meant for me, was in his leg.

As I watched, he depressed the plunger.

CHAPTER SIXTEEN

A fter too much time staring at over-cooked-oatmeal walls, the color in my living room was a balm.

I sat on a velvet loveseat with Anarchy's arms draped protectively around my shoulders.

Mother sat across from us.

Charlie hovered near the bar cart.

Libba flitted. From the gin to Aggie's cheese board, and back again,

Beau sat on the floor next to me.

Grace stood at the window. "He's here."

We'd been waiting on Hunter. At Mother's insistence. Although, why she thought we needed a lawyer was beyond me.

"I'll get the door." Grace left us, and a moment later we heard voices in the front hall.

I reached for my iced tea, took a sip, and shivered.

"Would you rather have coffee?" Anarchy really was the perfect man.

"Not right now." Right now, I wanted to get this over with. Telling Mother and Charlie what had happened. How wrong I'd been. How I'd nearly gotten myself killed. "Beau, would you please take the dogs out?"

"May I do it later?"

"My daughter asked you to do something, young man."

He shook his head and said, "I'm sorry, Mrs. Walford, but I'm not going anywhere."

My brave boy had stood up to Mother. Politely.

I shot Libba a death glare. She should not have blabbed about John and the syringe. I expanded my glare to include Charlie. If he hadn't told Libba about John's attempt to kill me, she wouldn't have shared the story. Beau had been shocked and frightened. Grace, who was more accustomed to attempts on my life, was suspiciously nonchalant.

"You can stay, Beau." Anarchy's tone brooked no argument.

I would offer an abridged version of John's actions.

Mother pursed her lips, folded her hands in her lap, and crossed her ankles. "Children should do as they're told." She might have expounded, but Hunter stepped into the living room.

She stood. "Thank you for coming."

"Of course, Frances. My pleasure." He scanned the room. Looking for Karma?

Mother resumed her seat, smoothed the fabric of her dress over her lap, and said, "It appears a doctor in the cardiology department colluded with a hospital pharmacist to harm Charlie's patients."

Hunter's expression remained politely interested.

Mother continued, "Both the doctor and the pharmacist are dead."

Charlie poured himself a drink. A strong one.

"What is the hospital's liability?" Mother asked.

"May I?" Hunter nodded to a wingback chair.

"Please." I was a terrible hostess. "May I offer you a drink?"

"Nothing. Thank you." He sat, propping a leather briefcase against the side of the chair. "What's your plan, Frances?"

"We will contact the affected patients' families and tell them what happened, then we'll craft a press release, accepting responsibility." A lesser woman might have considered a cover-up. Not Mother. For all her faults, she would not shirk.

"I suggest legal counsel be present when you talk to families. Also, you'll want a lawyer to craft the press release." Hunter turned to me and Anarchy. "I assume you two discovered what happened."

I nodded. "John Abrams was disgruntled because he was passed over to become head of the cardiology department. He believed destroying Charlie's reputation would get him the job. He killed himself when he was discovered."

"What about Olivia?" Charlie's glass was already empty. He refilled it. "What was her role?"

Anarchy shifted next to me. "We picked her up at Rick Lawson's house. She does not appear to have any involvement with the murders."

Charlie snorted. "She tried to kill Libba and me."

"True. Will you be pressing charges?"

"Of course," Charlie snapped. "She nearly flattened us."

Libba joined Charlie near the liquor and rested her palm against his forearm. "Charlie, she's your children's mother. Think what this will do to them." She turned to Hunter. "Could we get a restraining order? Ensure she can't come near us again?"

Hunter nodded. "That shouldn't be a problem."

"And Lawson?" Charlie's voice was harsh. "What about him?"

"As far as we can tell, he hasn't broken any laws." Anarchy sounded deeply disappointed.

Charlie's face was turning red. Liquor? Righteous indignation? A combination of both? "He aided and abetted the woman who tried to kill me." The police had found Olivia's damaged automobile hidden in Rick's garage.

"He claims he didn't know what she'd done." Anarchy

KILLING ME SOFTLY 177

replied. "She told him she damaged her car in a rear-end collision."

Mother sighed. "Charlie." She turned until she faced him. "Would you please fix me a scotch and water?"

"Of course." He splashed scotch into a glass and brought it to her. Then he collapsed on the couch. Poor Charlie was having a hard time with all this.

"Rick was so insistent about my going with him when we were in the lobby. Are you sure he's telling the truth?"

"He says that was at Olivia's request. She wanted to tell her side of the story."

Maybe. "The kids. She went after the kids."

"She claims that was a misunderstanding."

I wasn't sure I believed that. I leaned forward and smoothed Beau's hair.

"We're getting off topic," said Mother. "Hunter, will you work with the hospital's legal team?"

"Yes, Frances."

"Excellent." She glanced at her lap. "While I believe we should be transparent about John Abram's actions as they affected patients, I don't think we need to mention Ellison's involvement."

Hunter nodded. "That won't be a problem. Abrams' crimes were discovered, and he committed suicide. End of story."

Mother nodded, obviously pleased. "Excellent. Thank you so much for coming." It was a dismissal.

Hunter remained in his chair. "There is one more thing."

Mother lifted her brows.

"I have some business with Anarchy."

He did?

Hunter bent and retrieved a sheaf of documents from his briefcase. "I spoke with the interested parties, and they've agreed to terminate their rights."

Next to me, Anarchy sat up straighter.

"I have the documents here. We'll need to file them with the court, then we can proceed."

My heart stuttered. Anarchy had done it. He'd talked to Hunter. And Hunter, being Hunter, had solved problems that had seemed insurmountable to me. Tears wet my lashes then ran down my cheeks.

I turned to my husband. "When did you—"

"Last week." Pure joy shone in his brown eyes.

"Proceed?" asked Mother. "With what?"

Anarchy reached down and pulled Beau onto the couch between us. "An adoption. Beau will officially be ours."

Mother didn't move.

I held my breath and wrapped my arms around Beau, ready to protect him from her acid tongue.

"These two—" she nodded toward Anarchy and me "—are nothing but trouble. Ellison attracts dead bodies and killers. And Anarchy lets her. Are you sure about this, Beau?"

He bobbed his head. "Yes, ma'am."

She gave a tiny smile. "Then welcome to the family. You may call me Granna."

ALSO BY JULIE MULHERN

The Country Club Murders

The Deep End

Guaranteed to Bleed

Clouds in My Coffee

Send in the Clowns

Watching the Detectives

Cold as Ice

Shadow Dancing

Back Stabbers

Telephone Line

Stayin' Alive

Killer Queen

Night Moves

Lyin' Eyes

Big Shot

Fire and Rain

Killing Me Softly

The Poppy Fields Adventures

Fields' Guide to Abduction

Fields' Guide to Assassins

Fields' Guide to Voodoo

Fields' Guide to Fog

Fields' Guide to Pharaohs

Made in the USA
Coppell, TX
13 December 2024

42400309R00103